'It was a certain kn_____
you made me melt._____
is too important to _____

'I couldn't help _____
or now,' Johnny smiled, staring deeply into her eyes.

'You're doing it again, Johnny,' Delia laughed playfully, pulling him close to her.

'Good!' Johnny laughed too, as she put her arms around him, stared into his eyes with a moment's hesitation, and then kissed him hard and passionately.

'Oh, Delia,' Johnny cried, returning the passion.

They hugged and kissed under the huge swaying willow trees.

Also available and published by Bantam Books:

BABY, IT'S YOU
HELLO, STRANGER
BREAKING UP IS HARD TO DO

Save The Last Dance For Me

N.H. KLEINBAUM

Dirty Dancing ™

BANTAM BOOKS

TORONTO · NEW YORK · LONDON · SYDNEY · AUCKLAND

SAVE THE LAST DANCE FOR ME
A BANTAM BOOK 0 553 401203

Originally published in Great Britain by Bantam Books

PRINTING HISTORY
Bantam edition published 1989

TM and © MCMLXXXVII Vestron Pictures Inc.

Text copyright © 1989 by Transworld Publishers Ltd.

Bantam Books are published by Transworld Publishers Ltd., 61-63
Uxbridge Road, Ealing, London W5 5SA, in Australia by Trans-
world Publishers (Australia) Pty. Ltd., 15-23 Helles Avenue,
Moorebank, NSW 2170, and in New Zealand by Transworld
Publishers (N.Z.) Ltd., Cnr. Moselle and Waipareira Avenues,
Henderson, Auckland.

This book is set in 11 on 12pt Palatino.
Typeset by Chippendale Type, Otley, West Yorkshire.

Made and printed in Great Britain by
Cox & Wyman Ltd, Reading, Berks.

SAVE THE LAST DANCE FOR ME

One

'I can't believe I've only been here a few weeks,' Frances Kellerman sighed as she leaned back on the comfortable, padded lounge chair, stretching her tanned arms and legs.

'It's fantasyland here, isn't it, Baby?' Her cousin Robin laughed, calling her by the childhood name that wouldn't seem to go away.

Robin smiled, enjoyed the camaraderie she had developed with her cousin, and the leisure of her summer vacation as she looked around the green lawns and bustle of crowds at Kellerman's Hotel, her uncle's Catskill mountain retreat.

'I almost forget what my other life was like,' Baby chuckled, jutting her face up toward the sun.

'Maybe that's not so bad. I haven't really thought about school, studying and that empty feeling I've had for so long in the big old house in Roslyn since Mom and Dad's divorce.'

Her memory of her mother's recent visit to the hotel was still strong. She had come to celebrate her forty-sixth birthday. Initially Baby was eager to get her parents in the same place again. But her mother totally shocked her. She arrived, newly slim and attractive, determined to live an exciting life. She announced that she was selling the house Baby and her sister, Lisa, had grown up in and would be moving to a studio apartment in Greenwhich Village, in New York City. Baby's mother wanted to be where the action was!

Her initial anger and confusion over her mother's transformation was hard to deal with but now she was happy that they'd resolved so much. .

Baby felt good that her mother would try to establish a new life for herself after all. Everyone would be able to finally get along. She hoped that it wouldn't be so bad. It would always be different than before the divorce.

As she sipped a tall glass of iced coffee, she turned away from the sun and looked at Robin.

'You know, I actually *like* being a waitress here! It's fun. I've never done anything like it. I never really had to work at home. It feels good being responsible for a change.'

'*That's* a change I don't really want,' Robin answered, as she slurped a thick milk shake from a wide-brimmed glass. 'I like being here, away from my bossy parents, able to give Uncle Max moral support and watch you underlings see that everything is taken care of so all the guests are happy.'

Baby laughed. 'I can see that! You're good at knowing just how guests want to be treated!'

'Besides,' Robin sniffed defensively, 'I have to work on my tan and my tennis. I promised Mom I'd be ready to play at the club when the summer was over. At the rate I'm going, though, I'll just be a ballgirl, or whatever they call those people who chase after the balls at Wimbledon.'

'It certainly has been an incredible three weeks, though,' Baby mused. 'Being here with Dad, meeting people like Johnny Castle and Penny Rivera and the other kids. I've learned more here in such a short time – more than I ever learned in eighteen years living on Long Island.'

'It has been interesting,' Robin said, spooning a lump of ice cream into her mouth. 'Between your father and his romances, your mother and her lifestyle changes, and you and Johnny . . . '

'What do you mean, me and Johnny?' Baby snapped, interrupting her cousin. 'I told you, there is *nothing* much between me and Johnny. He's just teaching me to dance!'

'Thou dost protest too much, Baby dear,' Robin laughed. 'You might not want to admit it, but you've got a thing for that guy, even if he isn't exactly in "our league"!'

'And what exactly is "our league", Robin?' Baby shouted, jumping up from her seat, her face getting red with anger.

'Baby, wait,' Robin called. 'I didn't . . .'

At that moment a yellow cab pulled into the circular driveway of Kellerman's Hotel, not far from where the girls were sitting.

Baby walked up to the porch alongside Robin as the cab stopped. Both girls noticed the incredibly beautiful woman who confidently stepped out of the taxi.

Robin gasped as she noted the striking woman's long, lithe legs, dramatically shown to advantage in her red short shots, white and black tank top, and high, red backless heels.

The visitor put on a pair of black and white sun glasses, looked around, and started to walk up the stairs to the porch as the driver took her bag from the taxi.

'Hello,' Baby said, approaching the woman.

'Hi.'

'Welcome to Kellerman's,' she smiled, trying to hide how gawky she felt standing next to this sophisticated beauty.

'I'm Baby,' she gulped, feeling more like a twelve-year old than the boss' daughter or the welcome committee.

'They actually named you that?' the woman chuckled.

Baby blushed. 'No. My real name is Frances . . . it just never stuck the way Baby did.'

'I'll bet you're Daddy's girl, too?'

'How d'you know?' Baby looked surprised.

'Just a wild guess,' she said, extending her hand and flashing a warm, broad grin. 'My name's Delia. I'm looking for Johnny Castle. Do you know where I can find him?'

Baby gulped again. She'd just seen Johnny walk across the grounds toward the dance studio. He waved as he passed, causing her heart to beat faster, even though she tried, well, a little bit anyhow, to keep it still.

And now here was this gorgeous, leggy brunette coming to see Johnny. In spite of herself, Baby could feel her jealousy surface. She hated Delia even before she knew her, and thought, 'Looks like I won't have to worry about romantic attentions from him anymore!'

She smiled at Delia, hiding her own reluctant interest in Johnny. 'He's probably giving a lesson,' she said, matter-of-factly. 'He's the dance instructor here.'

Delia nodded, looking around at the sprawling grounds filled with crowds of bustling guests. Then she stared at Baby suggestively. 'Is he any good?'

Baby shrugged. 'He's all right, I guess.'

'All right?' Delia laughed, a sexy, throaty laugh. 'He must be slipping. I never heard anyone call Johnny Castle just "all right"!'

Robin coughed loudly and nudged at Baby's elbow.

'Oh, excuse me,' Baby said. 'Delia, this is my cousin, Robin Kellerman. Sorry!'

'How do you *do*?' Robin oozed, eyeballing Delia. 'Are you an *old* friend of Johnny's?' she asked, emphasizing the word a bit too strongly.

'Let's say we go way back,' Delia smiled. She turned and looked toward Norman, the bellboy, who had been standing starstruck staring at Delia ever since he spotted her on the porch a few moments before.

'So you girls are Kellermans like the hotel, are you?' Delia asked. The girls nodded.

'My Dad owns the place,' Baby said, feeling embarrassed. 'He took it over from Robin's dad a few years ago.'

Delia nodded as she continued to take in the surroundings.

'Do you take people's bags or just stand there thinking about it?' She pointed at Norman as she spotted him looking daffily delirious. He snapped out of an obvious reverie at the sound of her sexy voice.

'Bags, sure. That's my job. Sorry. I must've been . . . dreaming. No, I was definitely dreaming. You're Mrs . . . Miss . . . ?'

'Stone,' Delia said, ignoring the distinction, 'but Delia's fine.' She nodded toward her suitcase. 'Would you leave it in the lobby till I know if I'm staying . . . '

'Yes, sir, uh . . . Miss . . . uh . . . Miss Rock . . . Diamond . . . Stone,' Norman stammered, stumbling and bending next to her suitcase, unable to take his eyes off her legs.

'Can you take me to Johnny?' Delia asked, turning to Baby.

Baby hesitated. 'He usually doesn't like being interrupted when he's giving a lesson. He should be finished in . . . '

Delia smiled demurely. 'I'll make sure he doesn't come down on you for busting in . . . ' she assured.

'That's not the problem. I just . . . '

'You just think he's "all right"' Delia said with a knowing smile.

Baby gulped, caught off guard by this forth-
right woman. She walked down the steps.

'Follow me,' she called. Delia headed after her
with Robin excitedly in tow.

Baby walked ahead, leading Delia across the
hotel grounds toward the dance studio.

'Baby!' her father called, as he spotted her
walking with Delia and Robin. Max Kellerman
raced smoothly over to the trio and bowed
gallantly.

'And who is our attractive new guest?' he
asked with an interest that made Baby's face
turn red.

'Delia Stone,' the woman replied, reaching
out for Max's hand.

'How nice to meet you. Welcome to Kellerman's where . . .'

'Dad, this is Johnny Castle's *old* friend. She
came to see him. We're going over to the studio
now,' Baby interrupted, embarrassed by her
father's flirtations. 'Delia and Johnny go way
back,' Baby added, giving her father a 'get lost'
look.

'Ah, Johnny. A great dancer. Nice kid, too,'
Max said, taking a step back as he read the
message in Baby's eyes.

'See you later.' Max waved. He turned and
backed away. 'Nice meeting you, Miss Stone.'

'Delia,' she smiled.

'Delia.'

Baby turned on her heels. 'This way,' she said angrily as she raced two steps at a time up to the porch of the rehearsal hall. A Frank Sinatra record was just beginning to play in the background as they entered.

Johnny had his arms around a heavy-set woman in her sixties who was wearing tight pink pedal pushers and too much make-up. Her hair was done in a hairsprayed beehive, adding inches to her flabby five foot frame.

'Okay, Mrs Wolfe,' Johnny said, as he led the guest around the floor. 'Now you're getting it.'

Penny Lopez, the other instructor, was taking the male part as she tried to teach the steps to Mrs Wolfe's friend, Mrs Lister, practically pushing the oversized lady across the floor.

The music played and Johnny looked up briefly toward Baby and smiled slightly, still leading Mrs Wolfe across the floor. As his eyes met Delia's he stopped in his tracks and dropped Mrs Wolfe's arms.

The older lady stumbled in surprise when Johnny bolted from her side across the room to Delia.

'I don't believe it!' he cried, sweeping Delia into his arms and spinning her around with glee as Baby, Robin, Penny and the guests looked on.

He hugged her tightly, then held her back and looked straight into her eyes.

'How'd you find me?'

Delia laughed her Lauren Bacall laugh. 'I've got my ways.'

Everyone stood gazing at the gorgeous two-some in silence. Then Baby cleared her throat.

Johnny looked at the women watching him as though he was waking from a dream and suddenly remembered where he was.

'Uh . . . Baby, Penny, Robin, Mrs Wolfe, Mrs Lister . . . I'm sorry, excuse me! This is Delia.'

Mrs Wolfe sucked in her stomach and looked Delia's slim figure up and down.

'A pleasure,' she crooned with a strong Brooklyn accent, 'I'm sure.'

'We met,' Baby said shortly.

'Us too,' Robin echoed.

'Hello,' Mrs Lister gave a little wave.

Penny stood silently, angrily observing the electricity between Johnny and Delia.

'Duchess?' Johnny turned to Penny, oblivious of her dark, fiery eyes. 'Do me a favor and take over, okay?'

'Where are you going?' Penny asked pointedly.

Keeping his eyes on Delia, Johnny smiled. 'I haven't seen this lady in a lotta years. We've got some catching up to do.'

Mrs Wolfe smiled. 'So go. Catch up,' she urged. 'Aren't they cute?' she poked Mrs Lister.

Johnny put his arm around Delia, turned and walked out the door, leaving the other women behind.

Two

The pair walked arm and arm out the door and into the backstage area of the studio.

Johnny grabbed Delia and kissed her hard.

'I didn't realize how much I've missed you,' he sighed, as she smiled sweetly, admiring his tight, young body and muscular arms.

'I've missed you too, Johnny,' Delia said, taking him by the arm and putting further efforts at romance aside.

'Let's take a walk. It's hot back here.'

They walked out the back door across a broad expanse of beautiful green country grass.

Delia took a deep breath. 'It's beautiful here,' she sighed.

Johnny nodded.

'Must be wonderful to be here for the summer. Your waltz with that old lady was fantastic,' she said, trying to keep from laughing.

Johnny's face reddened. 'Hey, what is this?

You come here to see me or make fun of my job? I dance with the old ladies, it's not so bad. I also do my own stuff. Good stuff. Today stuff. I'm much better than my demonstration in there with Mrs Wolfe would suggest.' he said, defensively.

'I'd *never* say you weren't good,' Delia objected, pulling him closer to her. 'In fact, you're so good, you're the only one I feel I can ask for help. Because you're the only one who could do it!'

'Do what?' Johnny asked, looking confused. 'I thought you came here to see *me*?'

'I did,' Delia cooed, pushing him into a lawn chair secluded under huge willow trees and falling into his lap. 'But I also need to ask a favour.'

Johnny sighed, his face clouding with resentment, even though his body was responding to the feeling of Delia being so close.

'Sure,' he said, kicking his foot into the grass. 'What's up?'

Delia slid off his lap and moved next to Johnny. She animatedly outlined plans for a big upcoming dance contest in New York which she had entered with her teaching partner Raymond.

'So out of the blue Raymond calls me and says

he got a job at some fancy studio in Miami and he can't make it,' Delia concluded, looking at Johnny who averted her eyes.

'Nice guy.'

'Oh, you know dancers . . . can't depend on any of 'em,' Delia laughed. 'Anyway, this ball-room contest is the biggest in the country! Whoever wins it can call their own shots.'

Johnny looked at Delia, his eyes dark and hurt.

'I thought you always did that.'

Delia sighed. 'Johnny! Johnny! Johnny! I'm tired of moving around. I want to settle down, open my own studio in Manhattan. I can build up a clientele and still be near the action. While I'm still young enough. All I need is . . . '

Johnny lifted his head and looked into Delia's eyes. 'To win the contest. Right?'

Delia sensed his anger. She put her hand on his hair, stroking it softly.

'You're the best, Johnny. I should know. I taught you. But I need you to help me do this.'

'I thought you were here 'cause you missed me,' Johnny said, sounding like a disappointed little boy.

'Sure I missed you. We had a good thing . . . ' Delia started.

'We had everything!' Johnny said, grabbing her arms.

Delia pushed him gently back.

'Johnny. You were a kid. You know better now not to fall for an old bag like me . . . ' she laughed.

Johnny smiled softly. 'You were the best old bag I'd ever seen.'

'And you were the best thing that ever walked into the studio. I'll never forget the day you brought your kid sister in for lessons. I took one look at this big, sexy hunk of a guy – I knew I was looking at an incredible dancer.'

Johnny laughed distantly. 'You were looking at a lousy, misguided hood with a big attitude problem,' he said. 'If my mother hadn't done laundry so my little sister could take dance lessons, I'd never have met you. You saved my life . . . you know that?'

Delia grinned.

'Your mother didn't see it that way. What'd she say? "You stay away from my son and find someone your own age to drive crazy!" '

Johnny laughed. 'Something like that. Still. If it wasn't for you . . . '

Delia put her fingers on Johnny's lips. He kissed her hand.

'Listen, I have to tell you this,' he insisted. 'It's important to me. You're important to me. You always will be.'

Delia smiled.

'You showed me a world I only half knew existed,' he said, thinking back to his childhood in New Jersey, a family of eight cramped into a small, overcrowded house.

'The first time I ever saw a dancing girl was at Radio City Music Hall. My mother took me as a special thing when I was about ten. I used to deliver the washing and ironing she did to the fancy ladies on the other side of town.

'I'd seen those kinds of houses, from the front step anyhow. And I knew there was a better world. Better than the one we had. But when I went to the Music Hall and saw the dancing girls, the lights, the costumes, even the chandeliers and that incredible grand staircase, it was like a castle . . . a grand castle filled with music and beauty and happiness.

'There wasn't a lot of that where we lived, it seemed. The dancing was in the back of my head ever since then. I'll never forget it. But go tell my father the mechanic I want to take dancing lessons, right? That's all I had to do. I was either supposed to go to the Army like Richie, or be a mechanic like Frank, or work at the factory like my brother Joey. I couldn't even talk about it. Not to anyone except you. It wasn't cool to dance then. The guys would've called me weird. But then you showed me how wonderful it was, how wonderful I knew it would be. I owe you everything, Delia. Of course I'll help you with the contest. When is it?'

'Next weekend,' Delia whispered, touched by Johnny's memories and personal revelations.

'Next weekend! You've got to be kidding . . . I'll never . . .' he started.

'Shhh,' Delia said, putting her finger to his lips again. 'You promised to quit saying "never" on your sixteenth birthday . . . remember?'

Johnny's eyes clouded over and he smiled, almost blushing.

'I remember . . .'

'Great!' Delia said, jumping up and pulling him off the chair. 'I'll show you the routine.'

'Now?' he asked.

'Right now! We've got work to do!' She laughed, taking him by the hand, leading him back toward the studio.

'Next weekend?' Johnny repeated, scratching his head, 'Oh no!'

Three

That night, the dining room was filled to capacity, tables crowded with guests, happily stuffing their faces with the tons of food for which the Catskill hotels were famous.

'I'll have one of each,' an overweight Mr Schwartz laughed to José the attending busboy. Lester, the waiter, flinched at the thought of carrying all those plates of chopped liver, gefilte fish, matzo ball soup, broiled chicken, roast beef and more, not to mention the mounds of dessert, all the way from the back of the kitchen.

Making his way across the crowded floor to his station of eight tables in the dining room felt like running through a maze carrying an overweight frisbee. He shuddered for fear of dropping a tray every time he made the run.

'My luck to get tables of people who don't care how much they eat. Who got the dieters this week?' Lester whispered to his busboy.

José shrugged. 'I don't know where they put all this food,' he said, piling up the dirty dishes covered with leftovers. 'What's left could feed my family for a week.' He grimaced as he cleared the plates into a garbage can hidden under the tray station.

'They pay, they eat,' Lester smirked as he piled a selection of appetizers in front of Mr Schwartz and his family of equally big eaters.

'A little more bread, Lester,' Mrs Schwartz called. 'When you have a minute, dahling!'

Lester smiled and turned. 'When I grow two more arms and get a golf cart to the kitchen, lady,' he said to himself, as he lifted the tray overladen with dirty dishes and headed back toward the kitchen.

'José,' he called, 'See if you can borrow some bread from another table to satisfy these vultures until I get back.' The busboy winked.

'Sure thing, man,' he smiled, scouting nearby tables for an extra basket of bread rolls.

Over the din of moving dishes and chomping mouths, Sweets the pianist played soft dinner music at the front of the huge, sprawling dining hall.

Baby and Robin walked into the dining room and sat at their regular table.

'Boy, I'm exhausted,' Baby said, sitting down next to Robin. She wore a pink and white dinner dress with a small flower print and little sleeves . . . 'I'm so glad I have tonight off. This was the busiest afternoon I can remember! It was so hot out it seems that everyone wanted a drink every second of the afternoon.'

She sat and picked at the chopped liver on her plate as Robin ate voraciously, wiping her dish clean with a piece of soft, yellow challah bread.

'Well, considering you worked so hard, you don't have much of an appetite,' Robin observed, looking at Baby's nearly full plate.

The appetizers were cleared and an over-ladened plate of roast chicken was placed before each of them.

'You want that noodle pudding?' Robin asked, sweeping it up into her plate as Baby shook her head.

'I'm tired, but not really hungry,' Baby said.

She sighed and looked around the room at the smiling faces, filling up on chicken and steak, potatoes and puddings and all making sure to 'leave room' for the famous Kellerman desserts.

'I saw coconut cream pie on the menu for dessert,' Robin said. 'I could kill for that stuff. Listen, just so I don't look like a pig, you order one too. Even if you don't want it. I'm sure I'll want seconds but I hate to ask for them. Especially when Steve is the waiter. He is so cute!'

Baby turned and looked at Steve, a tall, pimply-faced boy with brown hair and horn-rimmed glasses.

'Go for him, Robin,' she smiled. 'He's waiting for you!'

Robin blushed.

Just then Johnny and Delia walked into the dining room, sitting at a nearby table. Baby noticed that he looked especially handsome, almost like a prep school boy, in a blue blazer and light blue shirt with khaki slacks, his hair slicked back, his eyes bright and his face glowing.

Delia wore a slinky, suggestive one-shouldered dress which successfully showcased her beautiful curves and long legs. They sat leaning close together, oblivious of those around them.

'Could you die?' Robin almost choked as she stuffed a piece of noodle pudding into her mouth.

'Look at that body! And she's old!'

Baby looked and sighed dejectly. 'She's not old.'

'She's pushing thirty-five if she's a day,' Robin objected. 'But who cares? I should look so good at twenty!'

She finished off the noodle pudding and drained her glass of coca-cola.

'This is where my mother says something like . . . "God gave you a wonderful mind. You can't have everything." *Please*! Take my mind!' Robin groaned. 'Give me that body!'

Baby looked at Robin's chubby dramatic face and laughed.

'Robin, you are too much! Either Delia has the best metabolism in the world, or she doesn't eat noodle pudding and two portions of coconut cream pie!' she chuckled.

Robin's face dropped.

'It's probably the metabolism,' Baby reassured her quickly as Robin eyed the pie and dug her fork into the huge portion.

Baby passed her piece over to Robin and watched as Johnny stood up from the table and headed toward Sweets at the piano.

He leaned over Sweets' shoulder as he twinkled a softly melody. 'Do me a favor, pal,' he whispered to Sweets. 'Play that Mathis song I like.'

'Ain't that just a little bit old-fashioned for you, Johnny boy?' Sweets said, without missing a beat.

Johnny nodded toward Delia, seated at the

table. 'That's the lady I told you about. That's the song we used to dance to . . . '

Sweets shook his head and sighed. 'She's doin' it to you all over again, huh?'

Johnny's face clouded. 'Sweets . . . could you just play the song? Leave the psychoanalysis for later, okay?'

'You got it . . . ' Sweets smiled as he segued from 'Blue Skies' into 'Misty'.

Johnny returned to his table where Delia glowed remembering their song. The pair leaned close together, whispering to each other as Baby watched sadly from the sidelines.

Delia leaned over and kissed Johnny's ear.

'Look at them,' Robin gushed as Baby tried to stifle a blush. 'I have one guess,' Robin smiled.

'No, it's more than that,' Baby objected. 'He's different around her.'

'I'm telling you, Baby, it's sex. Pure and simple. Look at that glow in his eyes. From what I've read, there's just one thing that puts *that* glow in your eyes!'

'Robin, you are so . . . '

'What?' Robin interrupted. 'Realistic?'

'Crude!' Baby slid lower into her seat, feeling immature and prissy as she looked at the sexy dress Delia wore so successfully.

'Okay, it isn't sex. It's her nifty eau de toilette . . . ' Robin laughed as she pulled over Baby's pie plate and started to attack it.

'This stuff is great!' Robin bubbled. 'I have to tell Gino his baking is getting better and better.'

Suddenly Baby jumped up from her seat. 'I'm full, Robin,' she said, as she looked toward Johnny and Delia and felt her heart thunder. 'I'll see you at the show.'

She bolted from the table and ran from the dining room as Robin looked after her.

Four

The next morning, Baby walked slowly along the path from her cabin to the main house.

She was up early and had an hour before she had to be at her breakfast station so she meandered around the grounds. She felt her sneakers getting wet with the fresh morning dew and deeply breathed in the cool mountain air.

'This Johnny thing is ridiculous,' she thought to herself. 'He's a grown man and he sees me as a young girl. Even though I don't feel like a girl. I'm just not as experienced as some people. But when I look at him and Delia I know that I still am not the kind of woman he'd want.'

Delia. The thought of her made Baby tense up. Why did she feel so threatened? She didn't even really know why she was at Kellerman's. She'd said something about a dance contest and her needing Johnny to help her out. Baby knew they practised dancing almost all day yesterday.

She also knew that Penny was angry and jealous of the whole thing; that was easy to see. Johnny had dumped his lessons on Penny and ignored her while he entertained Delia. He probably hadn't spent much time dancing with the kids at the staff quarters last night either.

Still, there was something different and special about Johnny, Baby thought. He must have his reasons.

She found herself walking down near the lake where a foggy mist lingered over the still water. It was so quiet.

Baby sat down on a morning misted lounge chair and stared out over the water. She felt her uniform getting damp from the dew. But it felt cool and soothing. It was going to be so hot that day that she was sure she'd dry up fast enough, anyhow.

Suddenly, she jumped at the sound of footsteps in the grass.

'Hi!' a familiar voice called. She turned.

It was Johnny. Baby's heart raced.

'What you doing here?' he asked. 'I thought this was my private place.'

'Oh, I couldn't sleep,' she stammered. 'Got up early and I had time before my shift.' She paused and looked at him as he slid comfortably next to her on the lawn chair.

'You come here often?' she asked.

'Most mornings,' he said, nodding his head. 'This is the kind of scenery you can't get too much of after you've grown up in a crowded house in Jersey. This is like paradise. Tall trees, green grass, a lake with ducks. Sometime's I think I'm watching a movie!'

He put his head back, took a deep breath and closed his eyes.

Baby studied him as he sat silently, almost reverently, enjoying the silence, the occasional quack of a duck on the water, the whistle of the wind through the trees.

'Must be different to come up here after being a city boy all your life,' she said softly.

'Different isn't the word,' he laughed, opening his eyes and turning toward her.

'The first two years I worked at small hotels, joints really. But even that was a great escape from the city, from my father, the mechanic, who always gave me a hard time . . . it was an escape from real life,' he sighed. 'I don't know if you can understand that, Baby, can you?'

'There are pressures no matter where you come from,' she said softly. 'Me? I was lucky to live in a nice place and have most of the things I needed. But the pressure was still there. Be my Baby. My *perfect* Baby.

'And then there was the divorce. I knew it was coming, I guess. But I couldn't really believe it when my Dad left. My mother was devastated. So was I. Lisa was away at college so it didn't bother her too much. But then, nothing affects my sister, Lisa, but Lisa!'

She stared at the rippling water.

'I've always been shy, never really felt one of the crowd or anything. So I buried myself in books. I don't think I'm any smarter than any other kids, I just couldn't feel comfortable socially, so I took refuge in the library.'

'A looker like you!' Johnny whistled. 'Those guys in your school were jerks! You're a beautiful girl . . . er, woman.'

Baby blushed.

'No, I'm not just saying it,' Johnny said, looking at her. 'You have a special niceness, something that comes outside from inside. You do for people. Care about people. Baby, that's special. It's a lot more than being one of the crowd. And you have beautiful eyes and a wonderful face. Those people on Long Island were jerks. And I thought Jersey was bad!'

Baby started laughing, doubling over in a hard belly laugh that brought tears to her eyes and made her abdomen ache.

'Johnny, that's probably the nicest thing

anybody ever said to me,' she sputtered between giggles. 'I really needed a laugh like that!'

'Yeah?' he asked. 'So what's with the laughing?'

'I was just picturing you at Roslyn High,' she smiled. 'You'd have no trouble being one of the gang. The girls would swoon.'

'Swoon, huh?' he smiled. 'Couldn't be too bad a place!'

Baby looked down at her watch. 'Oh my gosh!' she jumped up. 'It's 7.30! I've got to dash!'

'Yeah, me too!' Johnny jumped up from the lounge chair. 'Got to meet Delia for an early rehearsal.'

'You two are really busy with this contest thing,' Baby said, as they walked back toward the dining room.

'Well, it means a lot to her and she was there for me when I needed someone,' Johnny said. 'That's what friends are for.'

'You're right!' Baby smiled. She looked at Johnny and suddenly felt better about Delia's visit and the dance contest. 'Have a good rehearsal!'

She ran along the pathway into the dining room and began taking orders from the always hungry breakfast crowd.

The early risers were always the most hungry ones and Baby made several runs back and forth to the dining room with trays of fruit, juices, hot and cold cereals, and special order omelettes.

'Baby,' Mrs Breene called as Baby was sliding around the table, balancing three hot dishes, 'Some more cream cheese and lox for my bagels, honey. And a little of that delicious whitefish we had yesterday.'

'Sure thing, Mrs Breene,' Baby smiled, as she put down the dishes and lifted a tray loaded with dirty dishes. 'Be right back.'

As she headed toward the kitchen, she spotted her father talking to Johnny, waving a finger angrily in Johnny's face. Johnny nodded, standing silently.

Baby ran back to the kitchen, grabbed the food for Mrs Breene and delivered it to her station. She watched her father and Johnny out of the corner of her eye until Johnny walked away.

Max stalked toward her, mumbling to himself and shaking his fists in the air to no one in particular.

'Mornin', Dad,' Baby said cheerfully. 'Breakfast?'

'Hi, Baby,' he growled, giving her a peck on the cheek. 'Aren't you little Miss Sunshine today?' he said, pulling out a chair and plopping down angrily.

'You look more like a storm cloud,' she said, pouring him a cup of hot coffee.

'That Johnny, he's giving me an ulcer,' Max growled as he poured three packets of sugar into the hot coffee and drowned it with milk. 'I swear to God . . . he gives me a pain in my entire upper intestine.'

'I don't think that sugar and coffee will help, Dad,' Baby smiled. 'But what did Johnny do?'

'What did he do? It's what he didn't do! He missed three lessons with Mrs Wolfe. He's rescheduled Mrs Lister twice in two days! And then, then he has the nerve to ask me for three days off next week so he can go dance with that Ginger Rogers of his in New York!'

'Dad, it must be really important to him if he asked you,' Baby said.

'Don't defend his behavior to me this early in the morning! Please!' Max growled.

'Look, why don't you sip your coffee and I'll bring you some nice scrambled eggs and toast?' Baby suggested. 'You can't start the day on an empty stomach.'

'I don't have time,' Max grumbled, softening at the thought. 'Well . . . make sure they're well done? Okay? I hate them when they're runny.'

'You got it!' Baby smiled. 'And think about Johnny for a while before you say no. He's never asked for anything special before, now, has he?'

'Well, no, he hasn't,' Max mumbled. 'But, three days . . .'

Five

Later that afternoon, as Johnny and Delia practised their routine Penny and several of the girls watched from the sidelines.

'Okay, she's good,' Penny admitted reluctantly as she watched the fancy fox-trot routine, 'but I'm telling you, this is all she can do. This girl cannot get down! I mean, *anybody* can ballroom dance. Look at Mrs Wolfe. Even *she* can do it!'

The girls giggled at the image of Mrs Wolfe in her pink patio pants.

'You're right,' Lydia said. 'It's sort of like watching your parents at a wedding or something . . . '

'Must be embarrassing for Johnny,' Patsy added. 'This isn't his kind of stuff. It's so old-fashioned.'

Johnny and Delia danced as the music played on, her face the image of concentration, his distracted by her body and her eyes, staring at her and not paying attention to his feet.

He looked into her eyes, smiled, and suddenly lifted her and twirled her around for all the girls, including Penny, to see.

'Feels like old times, huh?' he smiled, enjoying the spin.

'Put me down. That's enough!' Delia's face was grim, her voice angry.

'It was never enough for us, Delia,' Johnny said, putting his arm around her waist.

'Put me down!' she nearly shouted. 'This isn't in the routine.' She glanced instantly at Penny and the other girls who watched with heightened interest.

'Or do you always have to show off in front of the girls?'

'Gimme a break! If this were any easier I'd be in a coma,' he snickered.

'Then why aren't you getting it?' she asked sarcastically.

'I'll get it,' Johnny sulked.

'When? We only have a couple of days!'

Johnny felt his anger rising. 'So let's stop talking and do it!' he said, putting a new record on the phonograph.

Penny and the girls watched for a while, then straggled out of the rehearsal hall bored by the show.

'Now that we're alone I hope you're going to concentrate!' Delia shouted. 'I notice that your fan club left!'

'That's not fair, Delia,' Johnny said, muffling his voice. 'I'm giving this my best shot. Let's call it quits. Maybe we need to split for a while.

'See you for dinner?' she asked.

'Nah. I'm grabbing a pizza with the guys in the staff house. See ya!' He turned and walked out of the hall, slamming the door behind him.

'He sure does look like a man, but he still acts like a boy,' Delia said, as she took the record off the machine and headed back to her room.

After the dinner rush that night, Baby was perched on a wooden table in the kichen filling salt and pepper shakers while Robin shoveled a huge plate of pie *à la mode* into her mouth.

'Thanks for keeping me company, Rob,' Baby said. 'I hate this job. I'm always afraid I'll forget which is which or mix up the salt and pepper together.'

'Forget it,' Robin laughed, not missing a stroke of dessert. 'It all goes down the same pipe anyhow. Force of habit. Most people who put on salt, automatically throw on some pepper.'

She stopped, her fork in mid-air. 'Actually, that might be a good invention, a combination of salt *and* pepper, pre-mixed. We could call it *palt* or *sepper*. Patent it and we could make a fortune. What do you think?'

'I think I better concentrate on which goes where right now, before you start spending those millions,' Baby laughed. 'Palt or sepper? Robin, you are too much!'

The door to the kitchen swung open and Delia walked in as the cousins were laughing.

'Private party or can anyone come in?' she asked.

One look at Delia's slinky, low-cut red dress and Robin put down her plate of fattening dessert. She gulped as she eyeballed Delia from her glistening head to the tip of her spiked heel toe.

'Where is everybody?' Delia asked, looking around the otherwise empty kitchen. 'It's only eleven o'clock!'

'There's a charades game in the lounge,' Baby suggested.

'There's bingo if charades is too intense for you . . . ' Robin said.

Delia slid up on the table and crossed her long, perfect legs. 'So what do you kids do for fun around here?' she asked.

'Nothing! We don't have any fun,' Robin said

matter-of-factly. Delia squealed with laughter.

'Where's Johnny?' she asked. 'I know *he's* not playing bingo!

'Thursday night is game night so he and Penny don't have to dance with the guests,' Baby explained. 'He's probably in the staff quarters.'

Delia slid off the table. 'How do I get there?'

'Well,' Baby said, putting the last set of shakers back on a tray, 'It's not really for everyone . . . '

'We don't go there,' Robin said quickly.

'That's not entirely true, Robin. I've been there. But,' she turned to Delia, 'it is sort of off-limits.'

'I've had some of my best times off-limits,' Delia smiled, brightening. 'Let's go!'

Baby hesitated for a brief moment, then put down the last shaker and turned to Robin.

'C'mon,' she smiled. 'Let's go!'

'Like this?' Robin shrieked. 'Look at me! I can't go anywhere like this!'

Delia headed out the door, motioning the girls to follow.

'Always remember,' she smiled turning her head saucily, 'It's not what you wear, it's how you wear it.'

Robin grimaced. 'Easy for you to say.'

Baby pulled off her apron, straightened her shirt and followed Delia. 'Robin! Come on!'

'Oh, I don't know . . . ' she whined as she shook her head, got up from the table and reluctantly followed them out of the kitchen.

'Which way?' Delia asked when they were outside the dining hall.

'Over here,' Baby motioned, pointing toward the bridge which led from the guests' area, over a small stream, up a flight of stone steps to the staff quarters on a landing above.

'I hear the music,' Robin said. 'They must be at it.'

'Let's hurry!' Delia said, taking off her heels and running on the grass after Baby. 'This sounds like fun!'

They stopped at the foot of the bridge.

'Put your shoes on, Delia, there are all kinds of things wiggling around here at night,' she cautioned.

Delia made a face. 'Yuk! Thanks. Good idea.'

She slipped on her spikes and clip-clopped over the bridge, up the stairs and over to the staff quarters hangout.

Strains of a Motown song blasted through the screens. Delia, Baby and Robin walked up the steps of the porch and into the room, packed with sweaty, smiling dancers wiggling and jumping to the toe-tapping sounds. The trio stood on the edge of the room listening to the song and watching the dancers.

'I'm not comfortable here,' Robin whined. 'My deodorant is failing me, I just know it!'

'Relax, Rob . . . ' Baby smiled.

'How? I can't even dance!' Robin whined again.

'Yes you can,' Delia whispered to Robin. 'Anyone can dance!'

Robin stared at her and made a face. 'What is this, a new religion or something? Some people – like me – cannot dance!'

But Delia didn't hear Robin's protests. Her eyes caught Johnny and Penny dancing in the center of the room, moving, bending, undulating with a heat and intensity, an animalistic frenzy, as though he were trying to shake off his frustration and confusion and she was issuing a mating call.

Penny moved with him, jumping on his hips and wiggling to the beat. She jumped down and started pulsating and shaking to the change in rhythm as Johnny grabbed another girl, the heat rising, the dancing intensifying. Penny grabbed another boy and the gyrating got hotter, both couples moving as if in a contest to see which could be hotter and heavier.

Delia took it all in.

'Reminds me of the old days,' she said to Baby. 'I think I'm going to do some reminiscing.'

Penny and Johnny were back dancing together again, hot and furiously, when Delia walked over and cut in.

'Isn't this beat a little too fast for you, mama?' Penny asked.

'I think I can keep up!' Delia smiled, without missing a beat. 'Can you?'

Delia turned her attention to Johnny and started to dance the way he had not seen her dance at Kellerman's, the way they used to dance in the old days, slow, daring, dirty. Johnny responded to her sexy energy as the kids gathered around and watched, clapping and howling, clearly understanding from the way this couple moved that they had known each other very well. The staff was captivated. All eyes were riveted to Delia and Johnny. Baby stared at them with embarrassment and envy.

'My God,' she thought. 'If only I could do that with Johnny, right now, here!'

Robin stood mute, her mouth hanging open.

The music blared on as Johnny and Delia, seeming without effort, danced from song to song, slowly undulating, totally focused on one another, answering each other's moves in perfect synchronization as they let the music seduce them and seduced each other to the beat of the music.

Baby and Robin turned and walked out, the music still playing, Delia and Johnny lost in a world of their own.

Six

The next day began as a picture postcard day at Kellerman's. Bright blue sky, highlighted with whisps of frothy clouds, heightened the crisp colors of everything in sight.

The sun was yellower, the trees, greener, the lake water more sparking and the pool water a sharper chlorine blue.

'What a gorgeous day!' Baby sighed, relaxing on a large multicolored beach towel in the warmth of the sun.

'That sun's gonna roast you, Baby,' Robin warned as she coated her nose and lips with thick, white zinc oxide ointment. 'You'll be peeling like an onion.'

'I usually tan; in fact, I'm starting to get a good one,' Baby said. She sat up, leaning on her elbows and took a look at her cousin's face.

'Robin Kellerman! There has *got* to be some other, less obvious way to protect your nose and lips,' Baby laughed. 'You look like you're ready for the circus!'

Robin's eyes welled with tears.

'Well, I don't tan,' she almost cried. 'I just burn. Burn and peel, burn and peel. It's so ugly and it hurts. There's nothing I can do!' she practically shouted. 'The circus! Thanks a lot!'

'Here, put on my hat,' Baby said. 'And calm down, I didn't mean to upset you. It's just you can't see how cute you are with all that white gunk on.'

Robin sniffed. 'You really think I'm cute?' she asked, tissuing the ointment off and hiding under the brim of the big straw hat.

'Of course you are, dummy. Didn't you see the way Steve the waiter brought you double desserts last night, without even being asked?'

Robin gave a small smile. 'That's true. Maybe there's hope after all. It's just there are so many beauties around here a girl could lose confidence, you know.'

The radio played softly in the background as the cousins talked.

'Would you turn that up a little, Rob?' Baby asked, as the Supremes' 'Baby I Need Your Lovin'' came on. 'I love this song.'

Baby swayed to the music on the radio.

'I sure would like to dance like Delia,' she

said. 'Johnny had started to teach me before Delia came. Then things got hectic and I haven't had much chance to work with him.'

'You were great in that first Saturday night show, though, Baby. You really do dance. You're better than you give yourself credit for.'

'Well, I like to dance. I like the feeling and all. But . . .'

'But I think you have to have a body like Delia's to dance like that,' Robin finished the thought.

'Mmm. You know, Rob, I think Johnny loves her . . . or loved her once . . . or . . .'

'What he did, Baby dear, is "did it" with her,' Robin said triumphantly. 'How much you wanna bet? Picture this. She was his baby-sitter and one afternoon when his parents were out and they were alone in the TV room . . .' Robin leaned forward on the blanket and acted out her theory 'She reached over and took him in her arms . . .'

'You're crazy!' Baby snapped.

'And then they melted together into the Castro Convertible. No other way two people could dance the way they did otherwise, Baby,' Robin said, as the two of them dissolved into a fit of giggles.

Baby took a long drink from her glass of lemonade and looked around at all the people sun-worshipping on the grass near the pool, and by the lake.

'Do you ever wonder when it will happen to you, Robin?' Baby asked. How? Who you'll be with?'

'Yeah, sure,' Robin said, sounding not quite romantic. 'And then I think that it'll be with some guy who still has braces and zits and my mother'll catch us, so I forget about it for another hour or so!'

Baby sighed, closed her eyes and lay back on her towel.

'I want it to be perfect,' she almost whispered. I want it to be magical and I want him to be sensitive and kind and . . . '

'Johnny.' Robin finished the sentence.

Baby sat up. 'You're wrong. 'Cause I want it to be forever.'

'With Johnny,' Robin said again.

'Will you cut it out?' Baby half-smiled, wishing it could be true. 'It could happen any time . . . do you realize that?'

'In my dreams, maybe,' Robin said.

'Forget dreams, Robin. We're growing up. We're ripe. We're ready. Pretty soon we'll know what it's all about . . . for real . . . !'

'Oh, my God!' Robin squealed, causing

several guests to turn and see what had happened. 'The thought of it is too much!'

Then Robin jumped up, trying to pull herself together. 'Get your stuff together. Fast! Let's go see if the kitchen's got any Rocky Road Ice Cream. Now that's reality and I'm having an anxiety attack at the very thought!'

Baby laughed. 'Robin, you are one in a million! Good idea.'

They grabbed up their gear and scrambled toward the kitchen.

While Baby and Robin found solace in a gallon of Rocky Road, Johnny and Delia were sweating it out on the dance floor of the rehearsal hall once again.

As they worked on a slow, romantic section of the routine. Johnny brushed Delia's neck with his lips, then leaned in to kiss her. Delia drew back.

'Come on,' she said harshly. 'We have got to get this.'

Johnny took a deep breath, walked over to the record player and started the music from the top.

'Fine,' he said. 'I've got it. What if it goes like this . . .'

With a fox-trot playing in the background, Johnny suddenly broke into a wild, interpretive version of their slow motion routine. He danced aggressively, twisting, bending, shaking and sliding to the routine.

Delia watched for a moment. She walked over to the record player and turned it off.

Johnny stopped dancing and slid into a sitting position on the floor, his face beaming.

'So, you think you have to be bumping and grinding to be dancing, is that it?' she asked angrily.

Johnny stood up, surprised by her angry reaction.

'Anything's better than a fox-trot around the room fifteen times! This is 1963, for God's sake!'

He leaned against the table, grabbed a towel and wiped his face which was dripping with sweat. 'Sorry, I just . . . I don't dance this way anymore, Delia. I took what you taught me, and I moved on. You should be proud.'

Delia's face tightened. 'I am proud. I'm proud, okay?'

Johnny looked at her tight-lipped expressionless face as he continued to dry off his sweat.

'I don't think you mean that, Delia,' he said.

Delia flung her arms up. 'I'm asking you to dance in one lousy contest!' she cried.

Johnny shook his head. 'It's not that easy, Delia! Yeah, I teach ballroom to the ladies . . . but I also work on my own stuff like I told you, like we did last night. I keep them separate. You mean too much to me to lie when I'm dancing with you.'

'Lie?' she shouted. 'Lie about what? What're you talking about? You're a kid from Jersey with a lotta crazy dreams in your head.'

Johnny's face turned beet red. 'Get this straight! I'm not a kid! Look at me – I'm ready for you, Delia. I'm who you always wanted me to be – don't you see that?

'In spite of my parents and the pressures not to be me, I'm ready for you. But maybe you're not ready for me! Cause my dreams *are* going to come true one day, even if yours aren't! With or without you, my dreams will come true!'

Delia stormed around the dance floor, her face flushed, her arms flaying.

'Well, when you've made it – when you're off somewhere with your name in lights – remember this, Mr Johnny Castle. You can talk down to me all you want – but I knew you when you didn't know the difference between a box step and a shoe box and you didn't know the first thing about how to talk to a woman or dance with a woman or . . . make love to a woman.

'I knew you then and I know you now and don't you forget it!'

The room was suddenly silent. The echo of

Delia's angry words bounced off the wooden beams. Filled with frustration and hurt, she stared and him, finally turned and walked out.

'Delia . . . ' Johnny called after her.

'Robin, let's go to the pool and swim off these ice cream calories,' Baby urged her cousin. 'The exercise is good for us. I have enough time before I have to set up tables and you have plenty of time before dinner begins.'

'It's not healthy to swim after eating,' Robin begged off. 'I might get a cramp.'

'Then you'd need one of the life guards, like Neil, to rescue you,' Baby suggested.

Robin considered this option momentarily.

'It might work if you weren't there, Baby, but Neil doesn't give me a second glance if you're around. I think the guy still is interested in you, even if he hasn't been making a really big play.'

'I told you, *I'm* not interested in Neil. I'm saving him for you, if you want him, of course. Aren't I a good cousin?'

Robin groaned.

'Gimme a break. After all that Rocky Road I need some antacid and a nap. Have fun. Swim five laps for me, Baby, okay?'

'See you later,' Baby waved, as she grabbed her towel and headed over to the pool.

*

She sat on the edge for a while getting her feet wet and taking Robin's advice about not swimming right after gorging herself with ice cream. Then she decided to take the plunge, walked to the deep water and dove into the pool, starting to swim laps.

Neil Mumford sat in the lifeguard's chair watching and commenting loudly.

'Your hips are rolling too much, Baby,' he called down, as Baby closed her eyes in embarrassment.

'That's better,' Neil called. 'Now kick harder. There you go!'

Baby finished her last lap, including five for Robin, and stepped out of the pool where her father stood holding a towel. He wrapped it around her, hugging her warmly.

'Thanks, Dad.'

'You know, Neil's right about your kick. You could work on it,' Max said, smiling up at the complacent lifeguard.

'What is this, an invitational swim meet or something? I'm just trying to get some exercise!' Baby said, exasperated.

She stood drying herself off with the towel as Mrs Wolfe, wearing lavendar pedal pushers and heels to match, clumped by.

'Baby, dahling, your stroke is improving. Much better. You looked very nice out there. Very nice.' She patted Baby on the back and walked along.

'Thank you . . . ' Baby said, not believing that what was supposed to be a simple swim had turned into a major commentary on her athletic prowess.

'I'm off to see that wonderful Mr Castle,' Mrs Wolfe smiled, turning back. 'We're working on my two step.'

'Have fun,' Baby said, waving Mrs Wolfe off toward the dance studio.

Mrs Wolfe walked off, practising the two step as she moved along. Baby plopped into a chair near the pool. Max walked over and sat down next to her.

'Well, I guess Mr Castle finally saw the light,' Max laughed.

'What light?' Baby asked, confused.

'The light that said, "Stop fooling around with some dancer old enough to be your mother and get back to work!"'

Baby's face was serious. 'Dad, I think they're in love with each other. You've heard of May-September romance.'

'Come on, Baby, that's not called love.'

'What is it?' Baby demanded.

Max sighed. 'It's commonly known as lust . . . and there's a big difference.'

Baby got up, wrapped herself in a towel and started to walk back to her cabin.

'You just don't understand, Dad,' she said angrily.

Max sighed. 'Oh, yes I do,' he said to himself. 'All too well.'

Seven

Mrs Wolfe two-stepped all the way from the pool to the dance studio, getting into the rhythm and looking forward to her dance lesson.

She saw Johnny waiting on the porch and waved. 'Yoo hoo, Mr Castle. I'm coming!' she called, demonstrating her technique as he applauded politely from the porch.

'Great Mrs Wolfe! Let's get started,' he smiled. 'You're making fantastic progress. Pretty soon you'll be on the staff with Penny and me.'

Mrs Wolfe pinched Johnny's cheek. 'Oh you silly boy! I'm not *that* good . . . yet!'

Johnny put a record on the phonograph as he and Mrs Wolfe began their dance instruction. Penny was working with another couple, painfully trying to master the cha-cha when Delia entered the room.

She walked up to Johnny while the music played.

'Could I talk to you for a minute, Johnny?' she interrupted.

Penny left her couple and stormed over to the record player, turning off the music.

'Why should he?' she asked harshly.

Delia turned to Penny. 'I'm talking to Johnny, young lady. Not you.'

'Well, why should I anyhow?' Johnny asked.

Delia turned and started to leave.

'Okay,' Johnny called after her, 'What is it?' he asked.

Delia stopped and turned back to Johnny. 'Could you just come outside and talk to me for a minute, please?'

He hesitated feeling Delia's gaze glued to his face as well as Penny's furious expression. Johnny took a deep breath and turned towards Mrs Wolfe.

'I'm sorry to interrupt this, Mrs Wolfe,' he said. 'You're doing great. Penny'll put the music back on. Keep practising that two-step. I'll be right back.'

She nodded and waved, keeping the two-step going without missing a beat.

Johnny followed Delia outside. She walked down a pathway near the rehearsal hall, out of the glare of the lights.

'You're right about the routine, Johnny,' Delia

began. 'It's old. But it's what they want to see, what wins . . . ' She paused and waited.

Johnny stood silently.

'I'm sorry about those things I said.'

'Which things, Delia?' Johnny asked angrily. 'You said a lot of things. Maybe you've been saving them up all this time.'

'No, that's not true! You *are* going somewhere, Johnny,' Delia cried. 'I can feel it. I always knew it and it's true. You're better than your teacher ever was, or ever will be. That's not an easy admission for a woman my age to make to a guy like you. But you're a natural. At everything, Johnny. You always were.

'I apologize, if I hurt your feelings. I guess I was angry because you rejected what I do and that hurt my ego.'

'I said some stupid things, too,' Johnny apologized, softening and moving closer to Delia. 'I guess I never got over you leaving me . . . the way you did. I was dumb enough to think you'd wait for me. You didn't even say goodbye . . . '

'I'm not very good with goodbyes Johnny.' Delia gave an apologetic smile.

'I did the best I could that last night we had together.'

'You remember that?' Johnny asked, astounded.

'What do you think I am, senile?' she laughed.
Johnny laughed, too.

'So, I don't get it then. Why have you been so
. . . like all business with me since you've been
here?'

'I didn't want to be distracted, Johnny. You
always distracted me . . . in the middle of the
fox-trot, for God's sake. It was a certain knack
you had . . . just looking at me made me melt. I
can't afford to give in to that now. This is too
important to me. It's my last chance!'

'I couldn't help myself when it came to you,
Delia, then or now,' Johnny smiled, staring
deeply into her eyes.

'You're doing it again, Johnny,' Delia laughed
playfully, pulling him close to her.

'Good!' Johnny laughed too, as she put her
arms around him, stared into his eyes with a
moment's hesitation, and then kissed him hard
and passionately.

'Oh, Delia!' Johnny cried, returning the passion.
They hugged and kissed under the huge
swaying willow trees.

'Oh my gosh . . . ' Johnny said. 'Mrs Wolfe is
still in there dancing with herself! I've got to
finish the lesson.'

'I'll be back later and we'll try the routine one
more time, Okay?' Delia asked, blowing him a

kiss as she ran across the grass back toward the main house.

Johnny waved. He took out his handkerchief and wiped off his mouth before heading back into the studio.

'Fantastic, Mrs Wolfe,' he called, as Penny glared from the other side of the room. 'You're so good, you don't even need a partner!'

Delia returned to the rehearsal studio late that afternoon and Johnny was waiting. They worked feverishly on the routine, repeating the same steps until they finally got it exactly right.

'It feels good, Delia. I know we're going to get it,' Johnny beamed as he hugged her after the final take.

'I knew you'd learn it Johnny,' Delia smiled. 'My star pupil!'

'Okay, one more time for good luck and then we're entitled to a long, cold drink,' Johnny said, as he replaced the record.

'Now, who's being the harsh taskmaster?' she smiled.

They danced around the room, dipping, twirling and bending in the 'old-fashioned' but elegant ballroom technique. Delia's graceful legs seemed to float along, Johnny led her masterfully, and they finished with a flourish.

'Cut!' Johnny called, kissing Delia in spite of his sweaty face.

'I'll take you up on that drink now,' she smiled, as they walked, arm in arm from the studio.

Cocktail hour began around 6 pm as guests, dressed in their evening finery, flocked to the lounge where Sweets sat tinkering on the piano.

Baby had the cocktail hour off. She would sit on the piano bench next to Sweets before changing into her hot, black dinner uniform.

Sweets played a series of slow, romantic tunes with Baby at his side, humming along. Several guests asked for special requests, bringing back old times and happy memories.

After the crowd thinned, Sweets turned to Baby.

'Hey, Baby, what's shakin'?' he asked, an expression of concern and understanding flashing across his face.

'Not too much,' she replied glumly.

'Come on now . . . something's got you down. Tell old Sweets about it. You're not too big for that yet?'

She shrugged.

'Couldn't have anything to do with our long-legged guest and Johnny boy, now, could it?' he zeroed in.

Baby sighed. 'Oh Sweets, Johnny's so in love with her! I mean, I can understand why . . . She's so . . . sure of herself and everything . . . '

'Uh-huh . . . ' Sweets nodded, listening.

'How do you get like that, Sweets? How do you get so confident?'

'Practise,' he smiled.

'I practise,' Baby confided. 'I really do. Sometimes I practise what I'm gonna say to someone over and over. I open my mouth – and the wrong thing comes out and I make a fool out of myself!'

Sweets laughed. 'That's how you learn, pretty girl. The more times you make a fool out of yourself, the easier it gets! Then it doesn't matter if you get laughed at. What's important is that you went for it.'

He paused, did a fancy finger run down the keyboard and finished the piece with a flourish. The guests applauded. Sweets waved and took a small bow.

'You know, it takes some living to get over this stuff. But, I know you, Baby. You'll get there. Trust Sweets,' he smiled. 'You'll get there.'

'When?' she asked impatiently.

Sweets laughed. 'In time, young lady . . . all in good time!'

'Thanks, Sweets, you're the best,' she smiled,

giving him a kiss on the cheek. 'I've got to change for the dinner shift. See ya!' She rose from the bench and walked slowly out of the lounge.

The dinner shift lasted almost four hours and by the end of the clean-up Baby thought she'd fall off her feet.

'I never made so many runs back and forth to the kitchen,' she told Lester as they headed out of the dining room after the breakfast set-up was complete.

'At least you don't have that Schwartz table,' Lester laughed. 'They're eating your father out of house and home.'

'My Mrs Breene does a pretty good job, too,' Baby laughed as they reached the path leading to the staff area and the road to Baby's cabin.

'See you up at the dance?' Lester asked.

'I don't know,' Baby sighed. 'My feet are killing me!'

'Forget your feet,' he laughed. 'Three minutes on the dance floor you'll feel like a new woman. Not that there's anything wrong with the old one,' he stammered.

Baby laughed. 'Maybe you're right,' she said. 'I'm going to freshen up. I'll see you later.'

She raced to her cabin where Robin was

already in her nightgown reading a movie magazine.

Baby took a quick shower as the radio played 'And Then He Kissed Me' and Robin sang along, totally off-key.

'You're killing that song, Robin,' Baby called from the shower.

'And you're raining on my parade, Baby. Let me at least enjoy singing to myself around here!'

Baby came out of the shower laughing, 'Sorry, you're right. You sounded great!'

'I didn't mean you had to get carried away . . . ' Robin laughed.

Baby put on a pair of sleek blue slacks, a pink t-shirt and was tying a scarf around her hair when she walked out of the tiny bathroom.

'So, what do you think?' she asked Robin, as she spun around for inspection.

'Dynamite! You look great!' Robin said. 'You sure you're up to this?'

'I'm really exhausted, to tell you the truth,' Baby said. 'But if Delia can just walk in there the way she did . . . so can I. You coming? You could change fast. I'll wait for you!'

'No way,' Robin shook her head. 'I'm still recovering from the other night when we went. You couldn't drag me in there. Besides, I need three hours to get ready, not three minutes like you!'

'Well, I'm going. See you later.

'Ta ta,' Robin called, as Baby walked out, slamming the door behind her.

Out on the patio, Delia sat alone at a table as a bellboy pulled a telephone over to her table.

She put the receiver to her ear.

'Hello?' she said into the phone. 'Raymond? What's up? Oh, fantastic! That's great! So we'll pick up where we left off . . . No, of course I didn't get anyone else. You're the only dancing partner for me. I'm just here for a few days' vacation. I'm leaving tonight so I'll call you when I get back to the city. 'Bye, doll!'

Delia put down the receiver, sat back and sighed, her face beaming. In the darkness she didn't notice Sweets sitting at the next table, his back towards her.

'Good news, Delia?' His deep, rich voice broke the dark silence.

'Oh, hi,' she stammered when he turned around to face her.

'You look happy,' he said. 'Must be good news?'

'I'm leaving,' she answered.

'Oh, I see. Does Johnny know?'

'Uh, not yet. See, I got my partner back. He's in from Miami in time for the contest. Maybe you wouldn't mind, uh, telling Johnny for me?' she looked at him beseechingly.

Sweets stood up, shaking his head. 'No ma'am,' he said sharply. 'That's not my job. Fact is, it's nobody's job but yours! You owe that much to Johnny, Delia, don't you think?' he said angrily.

Sweets turned and walked away, shaking his head.

Just as Sweets headed toward the main house Baby was walking down the path toward the patio. She stopped and heard Delia call her name.

'Baby! Wait!' Delia called.

Baby stopped as Delia walked quickly toward her. She wondered what Delia was doing alone out on the patio.

'Baby . . . ' she began. 'I'd like you to . . . to tell Johnny goodbye for me.'

Baby stared at her in disbelief.

'Goodbye? Where are you going? Don't you have the contest? He's been working like a dog to be perfect for it with you! Now you're running out on him? Why don't you tell him yoursel–'

'I don't have time,' Delia interrupted her. 'I don't even know where he is.'

'I'm sure he's in the staff quarters. The place we went to the other night.'

'Look,' Delia said, her eyes piercing Baby's, 'He won't understand. He thinks I'm someone else.'

'But . . . I thought you loved him,' Baby said.

Delia looked down for a moment, a tear dripping on one cheek.

'I'm doing the best I can, okay?'

'But how can you leave without saying good-bye? After all you've been through together?'

'Please,' Delia pleaded, backing away, 'You're his friend. It's better this way. Just tell him . . . '

She turned and ran down the pathway. Suddenly she stopped in the darkness and paused. 'Thanks, Baby,' she called. 'Thanks.'

Baby stood on the patio for several minutes, trying to figure out what had just happened.

Delia, the gorgeous woman she thought was so perfect, was too afraid to face Johnny and say goodbye.

She couldn't figure it out.

Sweets said it took living to learn. She certainly was getting some experience in living this summer!

She didn't know how to react to Delia's behavior. She couldn't deny that she was glad Delia didn't love Johnny and that she was leaving. But poor Johnny, how would he feel? Was she the one to comfort him?

Baby walked to the front porch of the staff dance room. She was surprised to find Johnny sitting alone on the steps.

'Hi,' she said, sitting down next to him.

'Hi.' He looked down at his boots.

Baby looked around, trying to figure out how to handle what she was left to do.

'Look, ah, Delia just stopped me. I met her on the path. She, ah, she asked me to say goodbye for her,' Baby stammered, trying to see Johnny's expression. 'She left . . . a few minutes ago.'

Johnny shook his head, stood up and turned his back toward Baby, gazing up at the star-studded sky.

Baby wanted to reach out and put her arms around him, but she stood still on the steps waiting.

'I tried to get her to stay . . . to tell you herself,' she explained.

Johnny turned around, looking at Baby. 'Nah. Not Delia. Once she's made up her mind – that's it. She's gone!'

Baby looked confused. 'I don't understand. You're not angry with her?'

'Sure I am,' Johnny admitted. 'But I knew

what I was getting into with her from the moment I met her . . . '

Baby listened, looking hard at Johnny's face, his moist eyes. He smiled at her slightly.

'You'll understand when it happens to you,' he said, awkwardly at first. 'I mean for the first time.'

Baby's throat filled and her heart pounded. Johnny looked deep into her eyes as he continued, talking both to Baby and himself at the same time.

'You're sharing yourself with someone in a way you've never done before. It's the best dance you'll ever learn, Baby,' he smiled. 'And the person you do it with will always be there . . . somewhere inside you . . . that's just the way it is.'

Their eyes met. After an instant, Baby looked away, enthralled and embarrassed by his honest, touching explanation.

She looked back at Johnny. 'Maybe then it is better to just remember her that way,' she said.

'Yeah,' Johnny smiled. 'I think so.'

The music inside the staff quarters was heating up. Baby and Johnny sat silently on the steps again for a few minutes, staring up at the peaceful night. After a while, Baby stood up and reached her hand out toward him.

'You coming in?' she asked Johnny.

'Nah . . . I don't feel much like dancing.' He smiled.

Baby kept her hand extended. 'C'mon, maybe there's a step or two you can teach me?'

Johnny laughed, stood up, took her hand, and led her toward the noisy room of dancers.

'Maybe so,' Johnny smiled, looking at Baby with new interest. 'Maybe so.'

'Besides, we have to practise for the big show this week, right?'

'Do you think your father will let us open for Bobby Darin Saturday night?' Johnny asked, getting back to reality at Kellerman's once again.

'Maybe so,' Baby winked. 'Maybe so!'

Eight

The anticipated arrival of Bobby Darin to head-line Saturday night's show was the big topic of discussion the next morning.

'I'm so excited! I've prepared a special menu of my original Italian dishes, just for Bobby,' Gino the chef told Baby as she loaded up her tray for breakfast.

'Not breakfast pasta I hope,' she laughed, as Gino grimaced and threw up his hands, turning his attention to the pancake batter.

Teenage girls were wolfing down less break-fast than usual that morning, anxious to be able to slip into their bikinis and bathing suits with hopes of seeing the famous movie and record star at the swimming pool.

'It's a madhouse out here,' Norman cried, as Baby raced past the main front porch with a special order tray for a guest who was feeling under the weather and needed 'cabin service'.

'It's Bobby Darin Fever, Norman,' Baby laughed. 'You just can't appreciate it if you're not a teenage girl.'

'That's not true.' Norman protested. 'I like Darin. I love the song "Mack the Knife". In fact, I do a terrific imitation of Bobby. That's the new addition to my repertoire,' Norman said, as Baby tried to get away, already late for another run inside the dining room.

Norman's comment intrigued her enough to stop.

'Your repertoire, Norman?'

'Yeah, thanks to your advice, Baby, I not only use my own jokes now, I'm working on impersonations. I do a great Nat King Cole, Johnny Mathis and my Bobby Darin is really pretty good. I figure I'll watch and listen to him this weekend, just to smooth over my rough edges.'

Baby burst out laughing.

'Norman, you are terrific! What a super idea. I love impersonators. I think you should also work on Sammy Davis Jr and Frank Sinatra. The guests will love it.'

Norman's face beamed.

'You really think so, Baby?'

She nodded as she moved toward the dining room.

'But stick to your plan and study Bobby Darin this weekend,' she said. 'He's really a hit!'

'Thanks,' Norman smiled. 'I will.'

He turned toward the hotel and began his imitation of Bobby Darin singing 'Mack the Knife'.

Suddenly, hordes of teenage girls came screaming in Norman's direction.

'Bobby, Bobby I hear him!' they shrieked, nearly knocking Norman down as they raced past him, thinking that the singer had been strolling nearby.

'Girls, girls,' Norman called, 'that was me. Bobby's not here yet!' Ignoring Norman's explanation, they ran across the lawn toward the tennis court.

'Must have been a good impression,' he chuckled, as he started to do a little 'Mona Lisa', *à la* Nat King Cole.

Norman waved as he saw Johnny and Penny walk toward the main entrance, talking animatedly to one another.

'Hi guys,' Norman called.

'Hi Norman,' they shouted back, without stopping to talk.

'You think he's gonna let us do it?' Penny

asked Johnny as they walked around the front steps of the main house.

'The dance?' Johnny asked. 'He better!'

'It's *so good!*' Penny beamed. 'He will. He has to.'

Johnny put his arm around Penny and squeezed her affectionately. 'You're my biggest fan, Duchess. Thanks. After the last few days, I needed that.'

'We all get our egos busted sometimes,' Penny said, thinking of her own jealousy over Delia. 'But that's behind you now. The important thing is to get to do the dance and open the big show for Bobby Darin.' She stopped in her tracks and turned toward Johnny. 'Just think, today the Catskills, next year Las Vegas.'

'Don't go getting yourself all carried away, now,' Johnny said, smiling at her enthusiasm. 'Although I'm not saying I don't like the sound of it. Vegas! God!'

Penny and Johnny walked past Max and Sweets sitting on the porch of the main house, overlooking the pool. They waved casually, trying not to show their anxiety and headed toward the dance studio.

Sweets sipped a cup of coffee and leaned back comfortably in a rocking chair.

'Listen Max. I know Bobby. He likes a warm-up

act. Gets the pulses moving, the crowds hopping, and then, *pow*, he jumps out and it's dynamite. And the women here love Johnny! It's a natural.'

Max rocked back and forth, looking at Sweets and listening.

'You know him, huh? Is he a nice guy?'

'Bobby? He's a sweetheart. And a pro. Max, he could be the best thing that ever happened to Kellerman's. And you make him happy with a great warm-up, he could become a regular. It would be great for business,' Sweets pointed out.

'Don't try to sell me, okay?' Max said testily.

'Come on, Max. Give Johnny a break. He's a great dancer. He even taught you the cha-cha,' Sweets laughed. 'I don't know many dancers who would attempt that!'

Sweets roared with laughter, nearly choking on his coffee. Max glared.

'All right, all right. He is a good dancer. And the ladies do like him. Sometimes too much,' he snarled.

'Hey, Max, get real. Don't go getting jealous over some twenty-year-old guy who works for you. He's a decent, hardworking kid and he could use a break. This might be it. It could help everyone.'

Max sighed.

'Besides, his mother's coming up this weekend. Give him a chance to show off. You had a mother once, too,' Sweets said. 'Didn't you?'

Sweets laughed and even Max's face cracked just a bit.

'Good, make me feel guilty,' said Max. 'Perfect. Next thing you'll be pulling out the American flag and apple pie.'

'Hey, some pie sounds good to me,' Sweets said, standing up and heading toward the kitchen.

Sweets turned and looked seriously at Max. 'All kidding aside, buddy, at least give it a look.'

'You got it, Sweets. Anything for you!' Max said. 'I'll join you for that pie.'

'You know, I hate the fact that you can eat all the sweets you want and stay so thin,' Max said, as he sucked in his stomach. 'Is that how you got your name?'

Sweets laughed. 'Come on, Maxy. You know it's 'cause of my sweet disposition. Sort of like yours, huh?' he laughed, as he walked into the kitchen.

Around the front of the hotel a car pulled into the circular drive in front of Kellerman's main entrance.

Squeals of joy from excited teenage girls surrounded the car. A shrieking group of young girls with autograph books leaned on the sedan, peering inside, in hopes of seeing the star coming to Kellerman's.

'It's just some regular people,' a chubby blonde called to the crowd.

'Let's go down to the gate, then we can see the car coming.'

'Great!' they screamed in unison and jumped away from the sedan, freeing the passengers trapped inside.

A man in his early fifties, craggy-looking and worn, got out from behind the wheel, stretched, and walked back toward the trunk of the car.

The woman, about forty-eight but looking older than her years, got out the passenger side. She stood silently and looked around, almost awestruck by the scenery.

Norman hopped to the rear of the car to help the man.

'Welcome to Kellerman's. My name's Norman,' he smiled. 'You gotta excuse the girls. They're jumping out of their skins with excitement because Bobby Darin is coming up today. I've been trying to keep them entertained myself, but they don't seem to like knock-knock jokes. I did give them a run for their money with an impersonation of Bobby though.'

'Here, lemme help you with those,' he said to the man and reached for the bags.

'I got 'em,' the man said curtly, grabbing tightly to the bags.

'Tom,' his wife said, 'let him. That's his job.'

'I got the bags,' Tom said harshly.

'Well,' Norman said, clearing his throat to break the tension, 'let's get you checked in. Mr and Mrs?'

'Callahan,' the wife answered. 'My son made the reservation. He works up here . . . '

'Callahan?' Norman looked confused. 'Don't think I know any . . . '

'Leave it alone, Margaret,' the husband said to his wife.

Mrs Callahan lowered her voice and whispered to Norman. 'He calls himself . . . Castle. Johnny . . . '

Norman's face brightened. 'You're Johnny's parents? Hey, that's great! I'll take you over as soon as we . . . ' He turned to Mr Callahan. 'Sure I can't help you with those bags, sir?'

'Yeah,' Tom said with finality. 'I'm sure.'

Nine

After their pie and coffee, Sweets and Max went to the rehearsal studio where Johnny, Penny and four other female dancers were preparing for the audition.

The men sat down and the music began, with Johnny and Penny, the featured dancers, enhanced by the pretty girls in a heated, Vegas-like routine.

Max and Sweets sat to one side, watching. When the dance ended, Johnny turned to Max.

'So . . . what'd you think?'

Max paused a moment, looking at the anxious dancers who stared back at him in nervous, sweaty anticipation.

'It's not bad,' Max said.

'Give 'em a break, will ya?' Sweets cried. 'It was dynamite! It was Vegas material. You were all fantastic . . . really terrific . . . '

'All right,' Max interrupted Sweets. 'Let's say it's better than I expected.'

'So, do we get to open for Bobby Darin or not?' Johnny asked straight out.

Max made a face and stared up at Johnny. 'Didn't your parents ever teach you how to get on someone's good side?' he asked.

'No!'

Max ignored the response and looked at the female dancers.

'So, what are these girls going to wear for this, er, number?' he asked.

'I've got that all handled, Mr Kellerman,' Penny said.

Max hesitated.

'Oh, all right. You're in . . . but keep it down to three minutes!'

The dancers hooted and howled as Max turned to leave.

'Mr Kellerman,' Johnny called after him. Max stopped. 'Thanks,' Johnny smiled. 'You won't be sorry.'

Sweets held up a V for Victory sign as Johnny and the girls hugged one another on stage and started to prepare for the big event.

Max nodded and left with Sweets. When they'd left, Johnny turned back to the dancers and raised his hand in a victory fist. The kids exploded with excitement.

'All right, everyone. I think we deserve to take five after this one,' Johnny called.

From the doorway, Norman and Johnny's mother watched as the dancers celebrated.

'Johnny? Hey, Johnny?' Norman called over their shrill laughter.

Johnny looked up to see Norman in the doorway with his mother. He jumped off the stage, raced to the door and lifted her in a bear hug, grinning with delight.

'Mom! God, it's good to see you!' he beamed.

Norman started to back out of the hall. 'Well, I gotta go keep Bobby's fans from getting run over,' he laughed. 'Have a nice day Mrs Castle . . . I mean, Callahan. Sorry.'

Margaret Callahan turned to Johnny, looked him over head to toe. 'You look skinny,' she laughed.

'I'm fine, Ma. How come you're so early? The train wasn't supposed to get in till five.'

'I didn't take the train,' she smiled. 'Your father drove.'

Johnny's face registered surprise. 'Pop's *here*?'

'He didn't want me coming alone,' she explained and then called out into the hall. 'Tom, you come in here now and say hello to your son.'

Johnny's father walked to the doorway holding a small package. He looked toward the stage and the dancers. 'I, uh, didn't want to interrupt anything . . . '

'I would've asked you to come too, Pop, I just . . . ' Johnny stammered.

'That's fine,' his father said curtly. 'I'm here now.'

The trio stood in uncomfortable silence for what seemed like a long moment until Margaret took the package from Tom and handed it to Johnny.

'I made it this morning,' she smiled. 'The soup you like. You could use a little meat on those bones. Even a dancer has to eat!'

Johnny's eyes felt wet.

'Thanks, Ma,' he said, looking at her tired face, her washed-out hair and plain floral dress. 'This is great!' he smiled. 'I've missed this soup!'

Margaret Callahan beamed. Johnny looked at his father who turned to go.

'Pop . . . '

Tom turned toward Johnny.

'I'm glad you came.'

That evening, the busboys decorated the main ballroom with balloons and sparklers for the special after-dinner dance.

Johnny sat with his parents at one of the small cocktail tables lining the walls.

'This place is beautiful,' Mrs Callahan said, looking around. 'It's so fancy. I can see why you like being up here.'

'The fancy part's not the only reason, Ma,' Johnny said, as his father puffed silently on a cigar. 'I give dancing lessons during the day, perform in shows during the week and dance with my friends up at the staff quarters at night. We're developing some exciting new routines.'

Mrs Callahan beamed with pride. 'I think it's grand, Johnny, just grand,' she said. 'Don't you, Tom?' She nudged her husband who didn't answer.

Just then, Baby, dressed in her waitress uniform, approached the table, setting drinks in front of them.

'Ma, Pop, this is my friend, Baby,' Johnny said, introducing her. 'I mean Frances. But everybody calls her Baby.'

'I'm glad to meet you.' Baby smiled warmly at the Callahans. 'If there's anything I can do while you're here, just let me know.'

'You're very nice, dear. Thank you,' Margaret Callahan smiled.

'Thanks, Baby,' Johnny said. His father lifted the drink and sipped slowly in silence.

Meanwhile, Max was working the room, moving from table to table and greeting guests, old regulars who had been returning to Kellerman's every summer for decades, and newcomers, whom Max viewed as the regulars of the future.

Baby smiled and moved from the Callahan table toward Max.

'Dad,' she hissed. 'You said you were going to say hello.'

'What?' he asked, smiling and waving across the room as he answered Baby.

'To Johnny's parents!'

Max looked toward the table and shuddered.

'I'll get over there. I'm working my way over there,' he promised.

'Now, Dad,' Baby ordered.

Max looked at her face and headed immediately for the Callahan table.

Baby stood back, watching him.

Johnny stood up, as Max approached. 'So, Mr and Mrs Castle . . . ' Max said.

Johnny flnched. His father stood up and offered his hand to Max. 'The name's Callahan. Tom Callahan,' he said brusquely.

'Of course, of course,' he stumbled, smiling at Johnny. 'I guess when you have a kid in show business, that's what happens. He changes your name on you,' Max bumbled.

'He didn't change *my* name,' Johnny's father said emphatically. 'This is my wife, Margaret Callahan.'

'Right,' Max said, uncomfortably, anxious to get away from the table. 'Nice to meet you. Well, you must be excited your son's opening for Bobby Darin tomorrow. He's a good dancer, huh?' he said, looking at Mr Callahan.

After another awkward moment, Johnny said, 'My father's never seen me dance.'

Max flinched, obviously caught up in more than he wished to handle. 'Is that so? Well, well . . . I hope to be seeing more of you. Enjoy yourselves.'

He backed away, wiping sweat from his forehead and headed toward Baby.

'Don't you *ever* do that to me again,' he growled through gritted teeth. 'They don't even talk to each other. The father doesn't watch the son dance. The mother sits smiling like a Cheshire Cat on a keg of dynamite. I screw up the name change and *you* want to make sure I don't forget to give them a big greeting! Thanks for nothing!'

Max stormed away sticking his handkerchief in his pocket and a big happy smile on his face. 'Mrs Walden, how beautiful you look tonight.

Ready for some dancing?' he oozed as he resumed his table-hopping.

Baby stared after her father, not sure what he had been talking about. But before she could even catch him, Sweets struck up the band and she went back to serving her tables.

'Good evening, ladies and gentlemen,' Sweets smooth, mellow voice crooned into the microphone. 'And now for your dancing pleasure, the boys and I are going to perform a little medley. Hope you like it.'

Sweets counted to the band and a fox trot began.

'Want to dance, Mom?' Johnny asked his mother.

'I'd love to . . .' she answered, starting to stand up.

Before he could escort his mother to the floor, Johnny was interrupted by one of his dance students.

At forty-five Mrs Roper, a svelte woman who was always looking for action, walked up to the table in a tight blue dress outlining every curve of her body.

'I think this is our dance, isn't it, Johnny darling?' she asked.

Johnny gulped. 'I'm afraid I promised this

one to my mother, Mrs Roper. It's my night
off.'

'No, you go. Dance,' his mother said, settling
back down into her seat. 'I'm fine.'

Johnny flushed as he felt his father's critical
eyes, then led Mrs Roper to the dance floor.

She nuzzled close to Johnny, holding him
tightly around the neck and doing a sexy,
intimate fox-trot. After a few minutes, Johnny's
father stood up.

'Where are you going?' his wife asked.

Without a word, Tom Callahan walked out of
the room. Johnny saw his father's face before he
turned to go. He took a deep breath, excused
himself from Mrs Roper and walked back to his
mother.

'Why did you bring him?' Johnny asked, as he
crumpled into the seat.

'You know your father. We go everywhere
together,' Margaret explained.

'He doesn't want to be here, Ma.'

'I want to be here. I want to see you dance
with Bobby Darin,' his mother smiled.

Johnny smiled back. 'Ma, I'm not dancing *with*
Bobby Darin. I'm just in the same show.'

'Well, he's very lucky to have you,' she said,
quickly adding. 'Why don't you go talk to your
father, Johnny?'

'It's not going to work. You always think it will . . . it never does.'

'Talk to him, please,' she pleaded.

Johnny sighed and headed out the door. His mother watched him leave, then turned to enjoy the couples dancing on the floor.

'My,' she thought, 'This really is pleasant.'

Ten

'Psst, Baby!'

Robin stood in the corner of the ballroom as Baby carried a tray laden with cocktails.

'I saw him! I actually saw Bobby Darin!'

'Not now, Robin. If I drop this tray you'll be seeing more than one star . . . wait until I finish serving. I'll be right back.'

Baby carried her tray to her station and served the pina coladas with orange slices and strawberries, tall banana daiquiris with tiny coloured umbrellas and shapely glasses of assorted wines and beers to her guests.

'Everyone okay?' she smiled, as she placed a bowl of peanuts on each table. 'I'll be back in a while if you need a refill.'

She took her tray and walked back to where Robin was waiting.

'One of these days Robin, I'm going to drop a tray and *you*, my dear cousin, will have to pick up the pieces. Why do you always hide like that?'

'I couldn't wait to tell you. It just happened!'

'What happened!'

'Bobby Darin was singing in the hallway! I heard him with my own ears. He's terrific! He was singing "Mack The Knife" as he kind of strolled down the hall. Funny thing is, he walked out the back door where the guests don't usually go. Maybe the performers do though . . . ' Robin mused as Baby burst into laughter, covering her mouth to keep from being heard.

Robin's eyes flared with anger. 'What's so funny? What now?' she demanded.

'Did you happen to see Norman a few minutes after you heard Bobby singing?' Baby asked innocently.

'As a matter of fact I did,' Robin said. 'He said he'd just spoken with Bobby and was going to get a record cover for an autograph.'

Baby ran into the kitchen, doubled over with laughter.

Robin stormed in after her. 'I do *not* like being laughed at!' she shouted.

'What's the joke?'

'I hate to be the one to tell you, Rob, but you *didn't* hear or see Bobby Darin singing.'

'But . . .'

'What you heard was Norman, *our own Norman*, doing his smoothed-around-the edges imitation of Bobby doing "Mack The Knife". It's part of Norman's new routine. He must have been practising.'

'How do you know, Miss Smartypants?' her cousin asked.

'Well, seems Mr Darin was tired from the trip up. He's just back from the Coast and really needed a good night's sleep so he called the front desk and asked if his dinner could be brought to his suite.'

'And who, pray tell, delivered that dinner?' Robin asked, her eyebrows furrowed.

'*Moi!*' laughed Baby. 'I saw Bobby Darin! He even offered me a $5 tip, but of course, I refused. I told him my father owned the place and all. He said he used to work as a waiter before he was discovered. He is *so* nice! And really good-looking. Although he did look tired.'

Robin's face was getting redder and redder as Baby filled in all the details.

'The one time it pays to be a waitress and I blow it!' she shouted, turning on her heels. 'Well!'

'You'll see him tomorrow night, Robin,' Baby called. 'He'll probably look even better in a tuxedo than he did in a bathrobe!'

Robin ran out the kitchen, slamming the door behind her. Baby checked her watch. 'Must be time for refills,' she said, clutching her tray and heading back to the cocktail station.

Anxious to please his mother, Johnny followed his father outside to the dining terrace. He looked around and saw him sitting alone at a small table, smoking. Johnny walked over to him.

'Mind if I sit down?' he asked.

'Suit yourself.'

Johnny pulled out a chair and sat across from his father.

'Dad, listen. Could we try and get along – for Ma's sake? I want her to have a nice time.'

His father blew a puff of smoke. 'So go be with her.'

'What is it with you?' Johnny asked. 'You're miserable so we all got to be miserable? Is that it?'

His father sat mute.

'Look,' Johnny continued, 'I know you don't like what I do here . . . '

'I wouldn't be here if it wasn't for your mother. She wanted to see you dance. So go and dance. Show her what you do for a living.'

'Are you that ashamed of me?' Johnny asked, staring at his father's cold, hardened face.

His father sat silent for a moment. 'I just don't get it,' he finally said. 'Why are you throwing your life away like this?'

Johnny took a deep breath and tried to get his father to look into his eyes. 'Dad, I love to dance,' he said intently. 'It's who I am. It's a dream I have. Maybe it seems a little out of reach . . . maybe I'll never really make it . . . but it doesn't stop me from hoping it'll come true some day. If I don't go after it now, I never will, and I'll always live to regret it.'

His father grimaced. 'You sound like a twelve-year old girl. Men don't talk like that.'

'Is that what you see when you look at me?' Johnny asked, bristling.

His father turned and looked out into the night, facing away from Johnny.

'What I see is my son being paid to pussyfoot around in tight pants with rich women. That's what I see! Does that make me happy? *No!* That makes me sick!'

Johnny's heart raced. His face flushed. 'You think if I'd stayed at home and worked in the garage with you all summer I'd be happy? Let me tell you something – that's the end of the road to me! Look at you!' he said, pushing his luck as he saw his father's back stiffen. 'Look at your life!'

'We have a good life!' his father shot back, turning to face him now. 'We worked hard – that's something you don't understand!'

'You don't have to spend your life under a car to work hard!' Johnny shouted back. 'That's something *you* don't understand.'

'Is that so?' his father said, puffing his cigarette.

'And look at Ma . . . ' Johnny's voice trailed off.

His father's nose twitched. 'What about her!' Tom shouted.

'What kind of life does *she* have? What good times does *she* have? Vacations? Never! Only work, work, work! The only nice times I remember are the times with Ma. No fights, no criticisms. She was the one who introduced me to dancing whether you know it or not!'

His father raised his eyebrows in disbelief.

'Your mother?'

'Not directly. But when I was a kid she once took me to the Radio City Music Hall. Took me where there was music and dance, grace and beauty. I was ten years old and I never forgot it.

'But what did she have for the most part? Work and more work? Home alone with five kids . . . taking care of everything by herself, doing other people's laundry at night. What kind of life is *that* to give your wife? That wouldn't make me proud. That would make me . . . '

Before Johnny finished his sentence, he felt his father slap him hard across the face. As blood trickled down the side of his face, Johnny stared up at his father, stunned and silent.

Mr Callahan walked away without saying a word. Several guests, aghast at the scene, rushed over to help Johnny. Johnny pushed them away, said he was fine, and wiped his mouth with a handkerchief. He stared grimly after the shadow of his father as he disappeared into the night.

Johnny walked back to his cabin, washed his face and examined his bruise. The cut was inside his lip, bloody but not too noticeable.

'That's the only way he knows how, is it?' he asked himself in the mirror. 'Fists, always fists.'

He put a cold towel on his face, took off his jacket and stretched out on his bed, doubling up the pillow to raise his head.

Johnny lay there for an hour, his anger seething, as the cool wet cloth brought some relief to his throbbing lip.

He dozed for a bit and woke up suddenly,

forgetting for a moment what had happened, until he spotted the blood-soaked towel.

He put on some Ray Charles music and stripped off his clothes. Standing in the hot shower, the water soothed his aching bones but not his aching spirit.

The music blasting, he put on jeans and a t-shirt and headed over to the staff dance room.

The room was packed, hot and humid, as the loud, intense music bounced off the walls, energizing the dancers who twisted, bent, leaned and shouted as they let off steam.

Johnny walked into the room and cut in on Penny who was dancing with another guy.

'Hi!' she smiled, over the blasting music, until she saw his swollen, cut lip. She reached out tenderly to touch his face, but Johnny pushed her hand away.

Both the music and Johnny intensified. He danced with dangerous energy, almost unaware of Penny's presence, angry and frustrated in a world of his own, trying to release it all on the dance floor.

Penny tried to go along with him, but stayed back, frightened by the way he was acting, wild and untamed.

Suddenly, Johnny stopped dancing, stalked

away from Penny and kicked open the screen door, ripping the screen. He ran down the steps and into the darkness as Penny stood helplessly watching from the porch.

'Poor Johnny,' she cried. 'Who can help him?'

Eleven

At 6.30 the next morning, Baby tiptoed out of her cabin while Robin snored noisily.

'She could sleep through an earthquake,' Baby laughed to herself. 'I don't know why I even bother to keep quiet!'

She walked briskly down the pathway, pinning up her hair in a bun as she went. The early sun went down, giving an indication of the sweltering heat and humidity yet to come.

'Morning,' she called to a couple of pool guys who were lining up rows of lounge chairs around the huge, glistening swimming pool.

'That water looks terrific,' Baby thought, pulling at the starched neck of her stiffling uniform. 'Boy, would I like to take a swim! I'd even practise my leg strokes for Neil,' she thought, smiling.

She stopped suddenly as the sound of 'I'm a Man' came blasting from the ballroom rehearsal hall; she turned and headed in that direction.

She skipped up the steps and peered into the hall. A single spotlight was focused on the stage where Johnny was working on his 'Vegas' dance.

He repeated one routine over and over again, trying to get it perfect, sweat dripping from his body, face drawn and tired.

'You look exhausted,' Baby said from the darkness, as she walked closer to the stage when the music stopped. 'Been here all night?'

Johnny walked to the record player and shook his head without answering. He grabbed a towel and dried off his face.

'I heard what happened . . . with your father,' Baby said, as Johnny put the music back on and continued to repeat the same single step from the routine.

'It's his way of communicating,' Johnny said, swinging around a make-believe lamp-post and hopping onto a nearby bench. 'He belts you. Not much you can say after that.'

'Are you all right? Your lip . . . '

'I'm fine,' he cut her off.

'Why does he—?'

'Hate me so much?' Johnny stood still on the bench staring down at Baby. He shrugged. 'He figures I ought to be more like my brothers. One's in the Army. My brother Frank works in the garage, Joey works at the plant with my uncle Rick. He's proud of all of them. My sister's still a kid in school. She's always been the baby princess, anyhow. But that doesn't bother me. She's a great kid. He's proud of her too. It's just me, always me. The dreamer. The one who wouldn't just take what was served up on the plate of life and accept it.

'He always seemed to resent that I wanted to go for more. And the dancing? To him it's for sissies, men who make money dancing with rich women. He told me it made him sick.'

'Oh no!' Baby cried, holding back from running to put her arms around Johnny and hug him. 'If only he could see you dance. You have a gift. A talent. Maybe your brothers just don't have that.'

Johnny laughed bitterly. 'My gift is to be the black sheep of the family, I'm afraid,' he said. 'Beside, it'll never happen that he would see me dance. It would make him wrong . . . and my father's *never* wrong!'

'Maybe it would help if someone else talked to him . . . ' she suggested.

'No, Baby. No. Don't get involved. It's my old man. It's my problem. I'm going to dance whether he sees it or not, whether he likes it or not. I'm going to dance because I have to!'

He turned the music up louder and jumped back to the routine he had been practising, executing a turn around his make-believe lamp-post when, suddenly, his ankle gave way under him. Baby watched, wanting to reach out. She stood silently.

Johnny stayed erect, avoiding her eyes, ignoring her presence, holding his balance, suddenly very still.

Baby couldn't stand it anymore.

'Are you all right?' she called out, starting toward the stage.

'Yeah. I'm fine,' Johnny said, motioning her away. 'I just want to work, okay?'

Baby saw him bite his lip and turn away.

'Oh sure, yeah, you must have lots to do,' she said. 'Good luck tonight.'

'Thanks, Baby,' he said softly, smiling. 'Thanks for always being here.'

She headed into the darkness toward the door. When Johnny thought she was gone, he limped to the nearest chair and slumped, down, holding his ankle, wincing in pain, as he eased off his shoe.

Baby held her breath as she watched, hidden in the doorway, glimpsing his moment of pain.

'Oh, Johnny!' she cried inside. She stood in the doorway as she watched him put an ice pack on his ankle.

'Why can't I do it? Reach out. He thanks me for "being here" but what am I doing? Watching him suffer? Hiding in the darkness? Why can't I go and be the one? He needs me now. Would he want me to?' Baby's thoughts raced in her head as she stood frozen in the doorway with Johnny only steps away. 'I know Johnny,' she said to herself sadly. 'He won't want help. Not unless the pain is unbearable. And even then . . . '

Baby stood tormented, wanting to reach out and afraid of being rejected. Finally, she turned and ran, her heart throbbing painfully, to the dining room.

Johnny rubbed his ankle which was aching and swollen. He hobbled in his sock over to the ice machine back stage and scooped out another bucket of ice, pouring it into his towel.

He stretched out on the prop bench with the ice pack on his ankle, feeling the pain slowly easing.

The anger and frustration of the fight with his father and the sleepless night of enraged dancing finally took its toll. Johnny fell asleep on the bench with the ice pack resting on his leg.

At 9.30, Penny came in to get ready for some final rehearsals and ballroom lessons she had scheduled that day.

She walked through the back stage door and was surprised to find a spotlight on.

Penny walked around to the front where the props were set up for the big warm-up number and there she found Johnny. The towel of ice had melted and a huge puddle of water was on the stage under the bench.

'Oh no!' Penny thought. 'That will ruin the floor! What happened? What is he doing here?'

Quietly Johnny slept as Penny ran for some paper towels and silently dried up the puddle of water.

Suddenly Johnny turned and sat upright, rubbing his eye. 'What the?' he looked around, trying to recall what had happened.

'You okay?' Penny asked, sitting in the front row.

'What are you doing here? What time is it?' he shouted angrily.

'I'm here to work and it's almost 10am,' she said. 'Now it's *my* turn for questions. What are *you* doing here? And what happened to your ankle that you needed a towel of ice? That stuff melts, you know. You nearly flooded the joint.'

Johnny jumped off the bench, his face contorting in pain. 'Oh my . . . '

'Johnny,' Penny ran onto the stage. 'What happened?'

'Nothing, really, I'm fine. I twisted it when I was practising this morning. I couldn't sleep so I tried to dance out my anger. I put the ice on to take away the pain. It helped the ankle, but not the rest of the pain.'

Penny sighed. 'I'm sorry. I wish there was something I could do about your father.'

'So does everyone,' he sighed. 'I guess I'll just have to learn to live with it.'

'Listen, you must know your part, if you worked all night,' Penny said. 'I'll work with the girls before my ballroom lessons, you take the morning off. It will do you good.'

Johnny smiled and hugged Penny close. 'Thanks, Duchess.'

He slipped his sock back on and carefully put on his shoe. He walked gingerly at first, fearful of stepping on the sore ankle. But the ice had helped and he soon was able to walk with only an occasional sharp pain.

'See you later, Pen. And thanks.'

She smiled and waved as the girls bounced into the hall, ready for rehearsal and excited about the big show that night.

'Where's Johnny going?' Gloria asked.

'He rehearsed on his own. I told him we'd do our own thing. Then tonight, we'll put it all together into a package fit for Bobby Darin!'

They giggled and cheered as Johnny walked out into the sunlight.

He slowly returned to his cabin and collapsed in his work-out clothes onto his bed where he slept for another three hours.

'Johnny?' There was a knock at the door.

'Johnny, it's me, Mother.' Margaret Callahan called as she pushed open the screen door.

'Ma!' Johnny said, sitting up in his bed, rumpled and weary-looking.

'Are you all right son? You're not sick, are you?'

'Nah!' he said, getting up out of bed. 'Just had a late night so I decided to sack out so I'll be ready for tonight. I'm fine. How'd you find me?'

'That nice Norman fellow, the one who thinks he's Bobby Darin, he showed me the way,' she smiled. Johnny laughed.

'It's a beautiful day outside. Are you rested enough for a walk?' she asked.

'Sure thing, Ma. Let me just wash my face a second. Sit on the porch. I'll be right there.'

'Fine,' she smiled, walking out and settling into the single rocker on the small porch.

Johnny went into the bathroom and threw some water on his face. He sat on the lid of the bowl and pulled down his sock to look at his ankle, now clearly red and swollen.

'Just my luck,' he sighed. 'I'm just going to

have to ignore it. I'm not blowing this one for ma, or Bobby Darin or *me*!'

He pulled on his shoes and met his mother on the porch, face freshly washed, his hair wet and slicked back.

'Oh, that's better,' she smiled. 'Let's go pick some wild flowers. There are so many of them here. It's just so beautiful!'

'Sure, Ma,' he smiled. 'Wild flowers are nice.'

They walked along a secluded path, Margaret carrying a bouquet of wild daffodils she'd gathered. Johnny was still wearing his work out clothes and the weary look had returned to his face.

'It breaks my heart to see this between you and your father,' his mother said.

'Ma, I invited *you* here. I just want you to have a good time, okay?' he said, wanting to avoid the discussion.

'I'm still hoping he'll come and see you dance tonight.'

'I don't want him there,' Johnny said bitterly.

Margaret stopped in her tracks and turned to her son.

'Now, Johnny, I agree that he had no right to hit you. But you must never attack him again about his life or my happiness. Do you understand? There are certain things you have no right to be involved with. He is still your father.'

'I'm sorry, Ma.'

They walked along in silence. She took him by the arm and led him toward a bench where they both sat down.

'There are things about your father you don't know. He stopped talking about it a long time ago, but he had dreams once, too, you know.'

'Yeah?' Johnny asked skeptically.

His mother's face brightened. 'Listen to me. Your father used to play baseball at school. He was the best . . . the best in the neighborhood. A scout for the Dodgers even came once. They told him he had a real chance to play with them.'

Johnny's eyes widened. His face filled with astonishment.

'But I thought he hated the Dodgers . . . '

His mother interrupted. 'I'm telling you, that was *his* dream. But he said "no". His family didn't have any money, your grandfather was sick by then . . . so he went to work as a mechanic instead.

'One day he saved enough to open his own garage, and we had our beautiful boys and pretty little Sarah. He took care of us, the best way he knew how. By then, baseball was a lost dream. But he had a dream, too!'

'The Dodgers?' Johnny repeated, trying to catch the full meaning of the story. 'I don't believe it.'

Margaret stroked her son's hair, wispy now from drying in the open air.

'That's because you're as stubborn as he is . . . The two of you . . . you're more alike than either of you know.'

She put her hands in her lap and look down.

'Do good tonight, Johnny. Even if he won't be there. Do good for me, huh? Do good for you.' She hesitated a moment, then added 'It's good to have a dream.'

Johnny's eyes misted as he reached out to his mother and hugged her close.

'Sure Ma. Thanks.'

Twelve

The excitement mounted all through dinner as staff and guests alike talked about the big show that night.

It was the first time a Hollywood star like Bobby Darin had played at Kellerman's and Max was as nervous as an expectant father.

He ran over to Sweets during dinner, too nervous himself to eat.

'Is everything all set?' he asked for the tenthousandth time. 'Music, sets, tables and chairs? The lights and sound systems have been doublechecked?'

'Max, Max Max,' Sweets laughed. 'Everything's been *triple*-checked! I just spoke to Bobby myself. He had an early dinner and he's relaxing in his suite. He loves the place. Raves about Gino's Italian dishes and is as happy as a clam. He'll be great. Johnny'll be great. Max, why don't you just relax and enjoy it? Then everyone will relax and we can have a good time.'

'Good idea,' Max said, mumbling to himself. 'A good time. We want to have a good time. He liked Gino's recipes?' he asked 'Good. Tell Gino. He'll like that. Wait! Don't. If you do, we'll be eating Italian dishes until they come out of our ears!'

'Max!' Sweets gave him a warning eye. 'Get lost and relax. Everything's under control.'

'Okay, Music Man,' Max smiled at Sweets. 'If you say it's under control, it's under control. But it sure as hell *better* be under control!'

Sweets laughed as Max walked across the dining room, nearly knocking over a young waitress loaded with a tray of dinners.

'Sorry,' he said, absentmindedly as he walked from the dining room.

After dinner, Robin and Baby dashed back to their cabin to freshen their make-up before the big show.

'That's enough eyeliner, Robin!' Baby called. 'You're going to look like Cleopatra.'

Robin came out of the bathroom looking very much like a teenage Cleopatra in pink chiffon.

'Dammit, Robin. I knew you'd make us late,'

Baby hissed, as they dashed toward the ball-room, walking tiptoe on the soft grass so their high heels wouldn't sink in.

'Well, I'm sorry, but it takes time to iron my hair and it needed a re-do,' she whined. 'And I did need just a touch of liner.'

Baby rolled her eyes.

Suddenly, Baby stopped as she noticed Tom Callahan sitting on the steps outside the ball-room, smoking a cigarette.

'Now look who's making us late,' Robin said, as she stared at Baby, oblivious of Mr Callahan and the situation.

'Go ahead without me,' Baby said. 'But don't forget to save me a seat. A good one. Right in front. I want to make sure I get a good view of Johnny's dance.'

'What's the matter with you?' Robin asked. 'You break a bra strap or something?'

Baby continued to stare at Mr Callahan. 'Ah, yeah, right. Go on. I'll catch up.'

'Oh, okay, but don't be too long. It will start soon,' Robin warned, lifting her long skirt and racing up the steps.

Baby crossed tentatively over to where Mr Callahan sat. She stood for a moment, contem-plating her words. She knew she'd promised Johnny she wouldn't get involved, but . . . She knew she had to do something. She hoped Johnny would understand if he ever found out.

'Good evening, Mr Callahan,' she heard herself say.

He looked up. 'Hello.'

'You're . . . going to miss the dance if you stay out here.'

He flicked his ashes into an ashtray from the smoldering cigarette.

'I'll live.'

Baby stood and looked across the lawn.

She could see inside the ballroom. People crowded around small cocktail tables that lined the room and filled the floor.

Margaret Callahan sat alone at a small table in the back of the room.

Suddenly, Johnny appeared in the doorway, still dressed in work-out clothes. He spotted his mother and, his head pounding with rage, took a deep breath, and walked toward her table.

'Get up, Ma,' he ordered.

'What?'

'I don't know who sat you back here but there must be some mistake. You're sitting up front.'

'Oh,' Margaret smiled, delighted, 'Well, that's a wonderf—' She stopped suddenly as Johnny lifted her table over his head and turned toward her.

'Would you mind bringing your own chair?'

'Oh, no,' she said, bewildered, as she followed Johnny who led the way across the room, finally stopping in the front.

'Excuse me, can you make some room please?' he asked politely. People squeezed out enough room for Johnny to put down his mother's table.

'Thank you,' he smiled to the guests.

'Sit down, Ma, and enjoy the show.'

She sat down, more than a bit self-consciously, as Johnny bent and kissed her on the cheek.

'Good luck, son,' she called, as he ran through the curtain backstage giving a small wave.

Outside, Baby stood awkwardly near Tom Callahan. They remained at a stand-off as Johnny's father lit another cigarette.

'Look, I know this is very . . . forward and all, and I usually don't . . . but . . . ' She hesitated and then blurted out, 'Why did you hit him?'

'What?' Tom said, taken aback by her forthrightness.

Baby felt her courage growing and her anger seething as she thought of Johnny dancing and his father punching his face.

'Did he do something so awful to you, just because he wants to dance?'

Mr Callahan's face turned bright red. 'Look: number one, it's none of your business . . . '

'Maybe you're right,' Baby interrupted. 'Maybe it isn't. But . . . he's your son!'

'An' number two, you don't understand.'

'What don't I understand?' she asked, refusing to give up. 'Just because he isn't doing things your way, he still has a right to . . . '

'And number three,' Mr Callahan said, raising his voice, 'learn some manners!'

He stalked away, throwing his cigarette butt to the ground. Baby ran after him, stopping to step on the still burning cigarette butt. She caught up to him and grabbed his arm.

Mr Callahan stopped and turned, amazed at this young girl who wasn't afraid to take him on.

When Baby realized what she'd done, she gasped, but only momentarily lost her fire.

'Now you listen,' she said, speaking rapid fire fast and in a tone so threatening that Callahan stood mute. 'I'm sorry, but . . . it seems so wrong that you've never seen him. I mean, he goes through so much sweat and pain to do what he does . . . He even hurt himself this morning after dancing all night because of his rage after you hit him. He tried to release that rage through dancing, rather than with fists.

'But he's not a quitter. He's still going on tonight. And he's going to be great. Because that's how much he loves to dance. And he'll be great whether you're there or not!'

'So let him,' Tom said. 'If he's so great he doesn't need me.'

Baby shoulders slumped. Her heart pounded. She felt she had failed Johnny.

'Don't you understand? Couldn't you just give him a chance . . . just this once? He's in the show . . . and you're here! All you have to do is take a few steps . . . a few steps to better know your own son.'

Tom turned from Baby, unyielding. 'I don't wanna see!' he shouted.

'Okay, fine,' she said, angry and confused. 'Forget it. You're right! You don't belong in there. In there is for people who care about Johnny! And that couldn't mean you!'

Baby turned in a fury and bolted up the staircase and into the hot, smoke-filled room.

Backstage, Johnny hurried up the stairs to the stage.

'Nice meeting you, too, Mr Darin,' he called to the star of the show who ducked into the one small dressing-room.

'Give 'em hell, kid,' Darin said to Johnny. 'I'm counting on you to get the audience hot!'

'No problem!' Johnny took his place in the wings. He quickly bent down to adjust the Ace bandage on his right ankle. Penny came up silently behind him.

'What's wrong?' she asked, a flash of concern crossing her face.

'Nothing. It's cool. Ready?' he smiled.

The music to 'Fever' filled every corner of the huge ballroom as Johnny and Penny made their entrance to a howling thunder of applause. Penny's brows furrowed in concern as she caught the occasional winces of pain on Johnny's face.

Penny and Johnny and the four female dancers captivated the audience with their show-stopping routine, but it was Johnny, who seemed to slide, turn, jump and glide effortlessly, who stole the performance. He was spectacular. Baby walked in and sat next to Robin, amazed as she watched the entrancing routine, especially after knowing how painful it must be for Johnny to move as he did. Even Max stood frozen, focused on the young talent, taken in by the quality and skill of his performance. The work had paid off and the audience roared their approval.

The dance was sizzling hot, but highly styl-ized and elegant. Johnny stood out in his all-black costume against the red swirling dresses of Penny and the other female dancers.

The dancers highlighted Johnny, who leapt across the stage, and slid gracefully to land on the prop lamp-post.

As he executed the turn from the lamp-post, leaping to a nearby bench, his ankle gave way, but his back was to the audience. Penny and the dancers saw the pain grip his face.

Refusing to give in to the excrutiating agony, Johnny forced himself back into the dance trying first one step, then two steps, his eyes starting to register defeat.

Suddenly he spotted his father standing in the ballroom entrance.

Electrified, he took a deep breath and picked up the dance with renewed intensity. Penny and the girls who had seen the agony cross his face stared at his magnetic performance in amazement and awe, as Johnny continued brilliantly.

The audience, never aware that anything had gone wrong, was dazzled, Johnny continued the routine to the final, triumphant climax. The audience erupted in ecstatic applause. The young girls in the audience, who had been looking for Bobby Darin, were shrieking and yelling for Johnny. Guests jumped to their feet in a standing ovation.

Johnny and the rest of the troupe bowed graciously, their faces beaming, their eyes twinkling. Penny glanced toward Johnny who was forcing himself to smile.

After three curtain calls, Johnny limped off stage with the help of Penny and the girls.

Tom Callahan stood motionless in the corner of the ballroom, taking in the pandemonium.

Max Kellerman stepped through the curtain after the dance was over.

'Thank you, ladies and gentlemen! A special thanks to our wonderful Kellerman Dancers, featuring Johnny Castle and Penny Lopez.

'And now, the moment we've all been waiting for, Mr. Music himself, Bobby Darin!'

The lights dimmed, the spotlight focused center-stage and the curtains parted as the real Bobby Darin started to sing 'Mack the Knife'.

Thirteen

Tom Callahan couldn't believe his eyes, or his ears. There he was, his kid, his Johnny, dancing up there as good as Fred Astaire.

Tom wiped a tear from the corner of his eye before anyone, especially that pushy little waitress called Baby, saw him.

He had to admit it, the kid had talent. Tom stood staring into space, hearing the melodious voice of Bobby Darin, another kid who wanted to be a star.

'I wonder what his parents said when he told them he wanted to be a singer?' Tom thought.

He looked toward the stage where Darin was singing, but all he could see was a re-run of Johnny dancing, sleek and elegantly, with the girls in the pretty red dresses.

'I guess it isn't all dancing with rich ladies. Maybe that's the hard price he has to pay to do the kind of thing he really wants,' Tom thought.

He slipped out the back door and walked along the pathway, over the bridge and toward the staff quarters.

In the background, he heard the hoots and howls of applause for Bobby Darin, a kid who'd followed his dreams.

'I think they were even louder for Johnny,' Tom thought proudly.

He stood in the darkness for several minutes just outside the screen door of Johnny's cabin. Tom took a deep breath and pushed open the door.

Johnny was lying on his bed while his mother, fluttering around like a nervous hen, rewrapped his foot in the Ace bandage several times. The pair looked up as Tom walked in.

'I can take care of this, Ma . . . ' Johnny said, looking up at his mother.

'You stay where you are, son. No moving. You hear?'

He nodded and smiled. His mother kissed him on the forehead and brushed back his hair.

'You were wonderful tonight,' she beamed. 'It was the proudest moment of my life. There you were, like Gene Kelly or Fred Astaire, as good as any of them. My Johnny. I was so very proud.'

'Thanks, Ma. That means a lot to me,' Johnny smiled.

Margaret turned and glanced at her husband, who had stood silently since he walked into the room.

Tom walked further into the room and stood still again, studying Johnny. Johnny didn't look up, although he could feel his father's eyes on him. He continued to wrap his ankle.

'I saw you dance,' Tom said.

Johnny didn't know what to say. He knew in his heart, that if he hadn't seen his father standing there, he might not have been able to go on. But he couldn't tell him that, Johnny knew. That's just the way it was. Tom crossed over to the bed and looked at Johnny's ankle.

'That was a stupid thing you did. You coulda hurt yourself permanent.' He looked down at Johnny's ankle.

'You're doin' that too tight.'

'I can handle it,' Johnny answered, feeling angry.

Tom's voice softened as he sat down on the bed. 'Let me wrap it.'

'Why do you even care?' Johnny said harshly, feeling confused and unsure.

''Cause that ankle's valuable. You're . . . kinda good,' he said hesitantly.

'Yeah?' Johnny raised his eyebrows in disbelief.

'Yeah!' his father smiled emphatically.

Johnny made room for him on the bed. Tom reached out and started to wrap the ankle, deftly and gently.

'So how 'bout those Dodgers, huh?' Johnny asked.

'They'll fold,' his father said matter-of-factly. 'They always do.'

'Guess you'd know,' Johnny almost whispered. After a moment, he looked at his father. 'Why didn't you tell me about that scout?'

Tom stopped wrapping for a second, looked up, then back down, and resumed what he was doing.

'Old news. Stupid stuff.'

'Stupid?' Johnny nearly shouted. 'It woulda been the biggest thing I ever heard!'

'What?' Tom said, trying to keep his anguish under control. 'That your old man wanted to be somebody special and it didn't happen? Busted dreams ain't worth spit.'

'Pop,' Johnny cried, 'you had a *shot*. Okay, so it didn't work out, but just for a minute, all the lights were on you. Some people, they wait their whole lives and they don't even get that!'

Tom grimaced. 'So I'm supposed to tell my

dreamy-eyed son I didn't get what I wanted? What would that do?'

'It would let *me* want somethin', too,' Johnny said softly. 'It woulda let me feel good about that. Make me proud to be a little like you.'

Tom looked down at the Ace bandage and continued to adjust it. He didn't look up at Johnny.

Finally, he did look at Johnny and smiled. 'I used to have a bum right ankle when I played ball. Guess it runs in the family! Well,' he said, patting the ankle gently, 'Guess we're all done here.'

'Maybe, Pop. Or maybe, if you want, we're just gettin' started.'

Tom looked at his son, his eyes misted over.

'Sorry I hit you, son.'

'Some shot,' Johnny laughed, rubbing his lip. 'Could you hit a curve ball that good?'

Tom smiled at him, holding onto Johnny's gaze.

After a moment, he stood up from the bed. 'Well,' he said. 'We're leavin' early in the morning. I guess I should turn in.'

He started toward the door.

'Pop?'

'Yeah?' Tom said, turning toward his son.

'Thanks . . . thanks for coming,' he managed to say.

Tom nodded and walked out the door.

'The Dodgers?' Johnny said out loud after his father had left. 'I'll be damned!'

Fourteen

Sunday dawned sunny, a perfect Catskills morning.

'Boy, I'm glad I've got the day off,' Baby sighed as she stretched out in her bed. 'I'm pooped. That show was so exciting last night. Johnny and Penny were so super. And Bobby Darin! What a dream boat!'

'It was great, wasn't it?' Robin said, quieter than usual.

'Robin, are you okay?' Baby asked, propping herself up on her elbow and looking across at her cousin's bed.

Robin was the picture of teenage magazine 'get beautiful fast' advertisements. Her hair was rolled in juicecan-sized rollers, her face covered with a white cream with tiny patches of Clerasil carefully placed over potential pimples.

'Robin?' Baby pressed.

'It was a special night,' Robin repeated, taking the rollers out one at a time. 'Baby? Can you keep a secret?'

'A secret?' Baby shrieked. 'You know I can. What is it?'

'It's Steve. I think I'm in love.'

'Steve?' Baby held back a giggle as she pictured the tall, pimply faced waiter who brought her toast and poached eggs every time she didn't have to serve breakfast.

'It was so romantic,' Robin said, wiping the white guck off her face with a wet washcloth. 'He held my hand and we walked in the moonlight. Out to the apple orchards. And Baby? . . . He kissed me! Under the moonlight, in the apple orchards, he actually kissed me!'

'Oh, Robin,' Baby smiled. 'That's great! I'm so happy for you. He's a really sweet guy.'

'Yeah, and cute too, in a funny kind of way,' Robin admitted. 'But there's something about him. When I'm with him I feel pretty and that means a lot to someone like me.'

'But you *are* pretty Robin,' Baby protested.

'Come on, Baby this is me, Robin. Look. I know who I am, pretty much, and what I am, too. I'm a girl who likes seconds on coconut cream pie, who can't pass a deep water test, and

will probably never get to play a complete game
of tennis.

'I'm also a girl who hasn't yet, shall we say,
"come into herself". So maybe someday I'll be
pretty, God willing, but right now, I'm a chubby
plain Jane who is deliriously happy to have a
guy actually interested in who I am right now.'

'You're very special Robin,' Baby smiled,
stepping out of bed. 'Steve is lucky to have
found you.'

Robin smiled. 'Yeah, I think so too,' she
giggled.

The girls dressed for the hot Sunday morning
and, for once, were ready at the same time.

'I want to meet Steve after he finishes serving
breakfast. Maybe he can help me with my tennis,' Robin said.

'Great idea. After last night, I want to go find
Johnny and Penny and tell them how great the
show was. I'm sure they've heard it a thousand
times by now. I thought Bobby Darin was great,
but I kind of expected that,' Baby said. 'But
Johnny was electrifying. He really took my
breath away.'

'Maybe he could help you with *your* tennis?'
Robin said pointedly.

'You goof!' Baby laughed. 'Go find Steve! I'll
see you later.'

They parted near the pool area where Baby spotted Max.

'Johnny was great, wasn't he?' Baby asked, as she caught up to her father, who was once again making the morning rounds and greeting the guests, preferably by their first names if he remembered them.

'He was okay,' Max said nonchalantly, as Baby stared at him, her eyes big as saucers.

'Okay, okay, he *was* great,' Max grinned. 'There I said it. Satisfied?'

'Only because it's the truth,' Baby smiled.

'Did you say goodbye to his parents? They were leaving this morning?' she asked.

'In fact I did,' Max smiled. 'Never know if a first-time guest will become a return guest.'

'That's the spirit, Dad,' Baby laughed.

'What's going on there?' Max asked as he pointed to a chorus of giggling Bobby Darin fans clustered around a chaise-lounge at the side of the pool.

'I chased those girls away before. We'll never get big-name entertainers if the guests keep harrassing them! Why can't they give Bobby two seconds of peace and a chance to relax by the pool?'

Max pushed ahead of Baby.

'Girls! Girls, now listen up!' Max called. The

fans looked in Max's direction, one young thing more attractive than the next.

'If you don't stop bothering Mr Darin right now, I'm going to have to ask you to leave.'

The girls started giggling and booing.

'But Mr Kellerman,' a tall, voluptuous blonde said, 'Johnny said he likes us being here. We're keeping him company!'

'I don't care what. . .' Max stopped in his tracks and pushed through the girls. 'Johnny?'

Max moved through the bevy of beauties and stared at Johnny Castle, holding court on a lounge chair by the pool, surrounded by cooing and giggling admirers.

Johnny lay in a bathing suit, looking tan and muscular, his Ace-bandaged ankle elevated on a chair.

'Mr Kellerman,' he greeted cheerfully, 'How are you?'

'What are you doing?' Max asked angrily.

Johnny pointed to his ankle.

'Recuperating, sir.'

'Johnny, honey, can I get you another drink?' a leggy brunette offered.

Johnny smiled and considered her offer, then handed her his glass.

'Sure. Why not?' he grinned.

Baby worked her way through the gaggle of fans, sarcastically evaluating Johnny's situation.

'Hurt a lot?' she asked pointedly.

'Gettin' better all the time,' he smiled broadly.

Max looked at the girls. 'What happened to you girls and Bobby Darin?' he asked. 'You've been dying to get close to him all weekend. How did he get away from you?'

'Didn't you hear?' the blonde asked Max, as she smiled seductively at Johnny. 'He left. Had to catch a plane back to the coast or someplace. So we'll just have to make do.'

She sat down to Johnny, nuzzling him on the lounge chair.

'Oh, Johnny baby, you're *so* brave!'

Max narrowed his eyes and stared at Johnny.

'You're going to need to be,' he sneered.

Baby laughed. 'Don't worry Dad . . . he can't keep it up too long.'

Johnny grinned at Baby, then back at the girls, and began singing his own interpretation of Bobby Darin's hit, 'Mack The Knife'.

He flashed Baby a brilliant smile.

'Better watch out for the sharks and their teeth,' she laughed, referring to the lyrics, as she pushed the blonde off the lounge chair and turned it over, dumping Johnny into the pool!

'I'm goin' to get you for this, Baby Kellerman,' Johnny shouted, wiping the chlorine water from his eyes. 'You just wait!'

'I'll be waiting, Mack,' she giggled, running from the pool. 'I'll be waiting for you!'

Don't miss . . .

Book Four

BREAKING UP IS HARD TO DO

Turn over the page for a sneak preview!

BREAKING UP IS HARD TO DO

Normally, to perform at Kellerman's was to perform with the sounds of talk, laughter, and the clinking of glasses as background accompaniment. Norman said that it was like trying to do your routine in the kitchen at home while everyone was having dinner. You were never sure if people were laughing at your jokes or because grandad's tie had fallen into his soup again. But tonight the ballroom was almost totally quiet. In the center of the stage was Danny Flare, America's Folk Singing Sensation, but he could have been the Pied Piper. While he strummed his guitar and sang 'Kisses Sweeter Than Wine' in his strong, clear voice, every eye was on him, every ear was straining not to miss a note.

Well, almost every eye, almost every ear. There were one or two exceptions, all of them leaning against the back wall, snickering.

Johnny leaned across Penny to talk to Bobby and Dominic. 'Hey, I know what,' he said in the loudest whisper Penny had ever heard, 'why don't we ask him to do "Whole Lotta Shakin' Goin' On".'

Both Bobby and Dominic thought this was as funny as Johnny did.

'No, no, I know what,' gasped Dom, 'maybe we could get him t'do, "He's a Rebel"!'

Penny gave Dominic a shove. 'Why don't you guys grow up, huh? And pipe down. I'm tryin' to hear the show.'

Johnny danced in front of her, making a face. 'Oooh, guys, Penny wants to hear the folk singer. She thinks he's a real humdinger.'

Penny moved sideways so that she could still see the stage. 'As a matter of fact,' she said, 'I do think he's good.'

Bobby pretended to barf. Johnny moaned. 'Aw, come on, Pen, you can't be serious. You *like* this guy?'

'Yeah, I like him. I think he's kinda cute.'

Johnny made a sound as though someone had just stabbed him. 'Cute? You think that nerd is cute? His teeth look like Chiclets. And look at that shirt. I bet his mother starched it for him.'

'Well, it looks to me like everybody else here thinks he's great. Except for you jerks.' She indicated the rapt audience. 'So why don't you all just shut up and let me listen?'

Johnny shook his head. 'You're kiddin', right? You can't possibly get off on this stuff. It's like college music, for Pete's sake. It's all nicey-nicey.'

Penny gave him a look. 'It's not all nicey-nicey. If you'd shut up for a minute and listen to it, you'd know that.' She punched him in the arm, a friendly punch by anybody's standards. 'Your problem, Johnny Castle, is that you just don't like anything you can't dance to.'

'And what's wrong with that?' Johnny wanted to know, bumping her hip with his. 'You don't usually complain about dancing with me.'

'Dance?' Bobby roared with laughter. 'About the only thing y'could do to this music is die.'

Dominic and Johnny cracked up at this. 'No, no,' choked Johnny, 'there's somethin' else you could do. You could go shopping.'

'Skate,' gasped Dom, grabbing hold of Johnny's arm, 'you could skate t'this great.'

Penny smirked. 'You guys are just jealous because there isn't a woman in this room who wouldn't like to trade places with that guitar.'

Johnny slapped his forehead. 'Oh, give me a break, will ya, Penny? Jealous? Of *him*?'

'Yeah, jealous of him.' She smiled sweetly, turning her head towards the center of the room. 'Little Miss Help The Poor seems to be enjoying this nicey-nicey college music all right. She looks like she's gettin' off on it just fine.'

Johnny followed her eyes to the table where Baby and Robin sat side by side, their attention given totally to the figure on the stage, their heads nodding in time to the music.

Penny watched Johnny watch Baby watch Danny Flare, wondering what thoughts were really going through his head. 'I guess,' she said at last, her voice as sweet as either wine or a kiss, 'I guess, it's your turn to be understanding, huh?'

Johnny leaned against the wall. 'Women,' he muttered under his breath. 'Who can figure them out?'

Robin stared at the stage as though someone had cast a spell over her. She hadn't spoken since Danny Flare first appeared. She hadn't once squirmed in her seat, trying to get a look at the eligible young men in the audience. She hadn't emitted one sigh because she was too fat, one moan because she had a pimple, or one grunt because her hair was limp. She had just sat in her seat, silent and immobile, the sub-urban teenager who was turned into stone while at a table at a Catskill resort, drinking a glass of diet soda. Or, to be more accurate, *not* drinking a glass of diet soda, since the glass in question had stood untouched in front of her throughout the performance.

Under her breath she sang along with Danny Flare, '. . . mmm-mmm . . . kisses sweeter than wine,' her eyes on his mouth, her imagination telling her just how sweet his kisses would be.

At last the set ended in a burst of applause, breaking the spell. Robin was clapping so hard she was nearly bouncing in her seat. Baby had to hold both their drinks to keep them from spilling over because of the shaking of the table.

'Encore!' yelled Robin. 'Encore!' Several people at nearby tables looked over at her uneasily.

Max appeared on stage, applauding and smiling at the bowing singer. 'Ladies and gentlemen,' Max beamed, extending his hand towards the man with the guitar, 'the folk singing sensation of the New Frontier, Mr Daniel Flame.'

'Flare!' shouted Robin, on her feet by now. 'Flare! Daniel Flare!' Several people at nearby tables who hadn't looked at Robin before looked at her now.

Max gestured towards Daniel. 'Let's give him a big hand, whatever his name is,' he smiled.

'Flare!' shrieked Robin. 'Daniel *Flare!*'

Baby tugged at Robin's skirt. 'For God's sake, Robin, sit down!' she hissed. 'Everybody's looking at you.'

'I don't care,' said Robin, reluctantly letting Baby pull her back into her seat. She was breathing hard and her face was flushed, but she looked happy. In fact, in the gentle light, her eyes sparkling with excitement, she looked prettier than Baby had ever remembered seeing her before. 'That was the most wonderful experience of my entire life,' sighed Robin, turning to her cousin. 'Oh, Baby, didn't you think that was fantastic?'

It's hot! It's sexy! It's fun!

Baby's life changes forever when she meets Johnny. For he is an electrifying dancer, and he shows Baby what dancing is *really* all about – the heat, the rhythm and the excitement . . .

A sensational series based on the characters from the top-grossing *Dirty Dancing* movie and television series.

Available now:

1. BABY, IT'S YOU
2. HELLO, STRANGER
3. SAVE THE LAST DANCE FOR ME
4. BREAKING UP IS HARD TO DO

Coming soon:

5. STAND BY ME
6. OUR DAY WILL COME